NEAR ENOUGH TO HOLD

A NOVEL OF LOVE LOST AND FOUND

KIM GOLDEN

JUST SO YOU KNOW...

Near Enough to Hold was previously published as a serial love story. This compiled version has been revised, edited, and contains new and expanded scenes.

For my friends and family whom I've lost between 2018 and 2021.
Each one of you touched my life in so many wonderful and
sometimes heartbreaking ways.
You are all missed.
You will always be in my heart.

PART I

NICK - SUMMER MOVED ON

1
_____

HERE COMES THE RAIN AGAIN

"Are you listening to me?"

Shit, I'd done it again—dazed out while my sister Ellie was talking to me. It wasn't intentional. I hadn't slept well in days, and she kept bringing up the past. I didn't want to talk about the past anymore. I rubbed my eyes with the back of my hand and muttered an apology. "Sorry, Ellie. What are we talking about again?"

"Boston," she said tersely. "I asked you if you're going to come home for Thanksgiving."

"That's months away." I kept my head down. An ant meandered between my feet. The back of my neck was sticky from sweating. I hated the end of August in Richmond almost as much as I hated thinking about going back to Boston. "Anyway, why can't you just come here?"

"I always come to you. It'd be good if you made an effort too."

We sounded like an old married couple. I lifted my head now and my younger sister's grimace was glaring. She was five years younger, but sometimes, it felt as if she was the older sibling. Especially lately. She took care of so many practicalities for me.

"Have you got your ticket?" I stood up and stared into the darkness. A lone train whistle sounded in the distance, most likely her train, the Northeast Regional that would carry her away from Richmond and whisk her back to Boston. She'd been here with me for two weeks and, as much as I'd enjoyed her company, I was ready to return to my normal life.

"Of course I have my ticket," she quipped. "I don't lose things."

"Don't be like this, Ellie." I turned back to her and ruffled her chestnut brown hair. She'd pulled it into a neat bun, just as she'd always worn it. I wished she'd let her hair down and stop worrying about me. "You know going back is hard for me."

"It's been five years, though."

"Doesn't mean it's any easier."

"It's never going to be easier if you don't face it."

Other passengers were venturing out now, jostling for the perfect position as they awaited the train's arrival. I grabbed Ellie's bags and moved aside. Ellie followed me. The air smelled damp and metallic. Soon it would rain. I could already feel its coolness in the thick air.

"Did you forget anything at the house?"

"You know I didn't," she said and touched my shoulder. "I just...I know going back is hard for you, but I wish my big brother would come and visit me. Everyone misses you."

"I know...I'll think about it."

"I'll even let you bring Rufus," she grinned. "He'll get his own room and everything."

"Rufus is a given." Rufus was a grizzled border terrier I'd adopted after moving back to Richmond. Sometimes I thought of him as my friend and savior. He certainly kept me sane in the early days. "Where I go, he goes."

"So, you'll come?"

"I'll think about it, Ellie. That's all I can promise right now."

"Okay," she conceded. "That's better than nothing."

The train pulled into the station and was loud enough to drown out any attempts at conversation. We said our goodbyes, and then Ellie hugged me so tightly I thought she would crack my ribs. "We'll see each other again soon," I promised her. "We'll be okay."

She nodded and kissed my cheek. "Love you, big brother."

"Love you too, kid."

I watched as she showed her ticket to the conductor and then headed across the tracks to the northbound platform. Thunder rolled in the whole night sky and fat drops of rain began to splatter on the asphalt. I didn't move. I wanted to make sure my kid sister boarded the train safely, and I wanted to see with my own eyes the train pull out of the station. So, I stood there, ignoring the snapping open of umbrellas and chatter of the others around me who were seeing off friends and loved ones. The signals clanged and announced the imminent departure of the Northeast Regional. As the train finally pulled out, I lifted my hand and waved. I could just see Ellie through one of the mottled windows. She waved back, her expression hopeful and heartbreaking.

Maybe she was right. Maybe it was time for me to go home.

The Staples Mill Road Train Station lacked the grandeur of the central train station in downtown Richmond. It had nothing going for it. Squat and square, bereft of anything attractive that made a person want to stay, no café, no restaurants, no bar. Maybe that was the point, though. Just drop off people and leave. I would have left immediately, but the rain was coming down harder now, slamming into the pavement and streets with a clattering ferocity.

"Do you think it'll stop soon?"

"Sorry?"

The woman standing next to me was soaked to the bone. Her dark hair hung in wet clumps; her thin dress clung to her body as a puddle formed at her sandaled feet. She was shivering.

"Do you think the rain will stop soon?" She rubbed her dark arms. Water dripped from her fingertips. "I was waiting for the bus, but it never came."

"The bus to town?"

She nodded. "I waited a while, but it never came."

"They canceled that bus. It hasn't run for close to a year now."

"But I checked online..."

"I don't think GRTC is that great when it comes to updating its website," I said with a shrug. Outside, the rain continued, rivulets of water ran down the windows and doors of the station. "Your best bet is a cab."

"I guess it is," she agreed. Her voice caught me. She headed for the door, dragging her wheeled suitcase behind her, and then went out into the rain. Three cabs were already pulling out of the station parking lot. I watched as she approached the two remaining cars. She must have sensed I was looking at her. She turned then waved. One less person to worry about.

.   .   .

I RAN ACROSS THE PARKING LOT TO MY CAR. THE RAIN WAS A torrential downpour now, and I didn't want to be out in it longer than necessary. I could already hear Rufus barking wildly. I'd left the window open so he could get some air, but Rufus hated thunder and lightning, and the air was already thick and charged. I was pretty sure the storm would get worse before it died down. At least there'd been no hurricane warnings. This was just your run-of-the-mill Virginia thunderstorm. Most likely, the rain would carry into the early hours of the morning.

I jumped in the car and patted Rufus on his scruffy head. "Sorry I took so long, buddy."

Rufus barked in return. He was shaking. The thunder must have ruffled him.

I started the engine and then braved the rain-slicked road. Beside me, Rufus whimpered with each burst of thunder.

"It's gonna be a long night, Rufus. Best get used to it."

———

"WHAT'S SHE DOING THERE?" I BLURTED OUT AS I STOPPED AT THE traffic light. The rain wasn't as fierce, but it still made its presence known. The woman I'd spoken to at the station was at the bus stop again. I pulled over to the side of the road. Rufus gave me a warning whimper. "Can't leave her out here when it's late, Rufus."

I rolled down the window. "What happened with the cab?"

At first, she didn't move. She stared at me without recognition. "I'm all right," she replied in a guarded voice. "The bus will be here soon."

"I told you before — they canceled the bus. You wait for it, and you'll be waiting a mighty long time."

She squinted at me. Her stance relaxed. "I didn't recognize you," she said. She looked worse for wear now. Her eyeliner and mascara were running down her face in black rivulets. "I didn't have enough for cab fare, and there's no ATM at the station. I figured I could start walking once the rain stops."

"You'll have a long walk ahead of you then," I told her. " You'd have to get on I-95 to get into town."

"Oh!" Her shoulders sagged. "I thought we were only a few miles from town."

"You must not be from around here then." I grinned at her. Rufus peered at her and sniffed her hand. "Where are you headed?"

"I'm supposed to stay with some friends on Ellwood Avenue. They were supposed to meet me."

"But they didn't come?"

"No, I waited for over an hour. Tried to call them..."

"What's your name?"

"What? Why?"

"If I'm going to give you a ride; I'd like to know your name," I said. "I'm Nick, by the way. And it sounds like you're headed to the Museum District, which is where I live."

"You'll drive me there?"

"Sure. At the rate you're going, you'll look like a drowned rat before you ever get there. So...what's your name?"

"Keisha."

"Well, hop in. Don't mind Rufus. He's harmless."

I popped the trunk and then got out and helped her with her suitcase. It was heavy. How had she even managed to pull this thing from the station? Once we loaded it in the trunk, I opened the passenger door for her. Her hair smelled like jasmine. The scent caught me off-guard. I nearly breathed it in and had to stop myself.

"I appreciate this," she said as she slid into the front passenger seat. "You saved my life."

At least there was someone's life I could save.

SHE DIDN'T TALK MUCH. MAYBE THAT WAS WHY RUFUS LIKED HER. He usually didn't like sharing the passenger seat with anyone, but he curled up in Keisha's lap, even with her soaking wet dress. She scratched him behind the ears and stared out the window, not saying a word until she saw the signs for the Museum District exit.

"You were right," she said softly. "I wouldn't have been able to walk it."

"Where are you from anyway?"

"Philadelphia. Well, not far from Philly—originally anyway."

"That where you're coming from now?"

"No, I was in London." She wiped her forehead with the back of her hand. "I'm a dancer. I *was* a dancer. But now I teach dance."

"That why you came to Richmond?"

"No, I came here for love."

"Love, huh?"

She nodded. "Someone I used to love. I think I still love him. We met up while he was in London for a book tour, and we decided to give it another try. That's why I'm here."

The way she said it was childlike. Her voice filled with wonder and joy. I smiled, remembering when I was once like that. Sometimes I missed it, that feeling of being in love, of being loved. Well, good for her. She had someone waiting. Even if the lucky guy hadn't shown up to meet her. Maybe she'd told him the wrong day.

By the time we turned onto Monument Avenue, the rain had stopped, and Rufus had fallen asleep in Keisha's lap. I made a left and drove toward Ellwood Avenue. "What's your friend's address?"

She fumbled in her bag and pulled out a soggy Moleskine notebook. She flipped it open. "3154 Ellwood."

3154? I glanced at her. "You're going to see Alex...?"

"You know him?"

I nodded. Everyone knew Alex. He was the local lothario. He was always hanging out in Secco Wine Bar, trying to charm women out of their pants and then ditching them when they got too clingy. "I've met him a couple of times."

"Small world," she laughed. "Once I'm settled in, you should come over for dinner. It'll be my way of thanking you for saving my life."

"I didn't save your life," I countered. "I just saved you from the rain."

"Same thing."

It didn't take long to come to Ellwood Avenue. I pulled up in front of the three-story, red brick house. A stubborn butterfly bush continued to bloom in the front yard despite it being so late in the season. Its lush branches and flowers blocked the view of the front door, but there were lights on in the upstairs windows. At least he was at home.

"Listen," I started, "if things don't work out, I'm just around the corner from here. My place is on Grove Avenue. I'm at 2811 Grove Avenue. Just come by. I've got a renovated carriage house that's sitting empty. You could use it if you need it."

"I'm sure I'll be okay, but I appreciate the offer."

"Well, the offer still stands. You need anything, just come by." I popped the trunk, got out of the car, and then walked to the trunk to lift her suitcase out and set it on the pavement. She was standing at the curb, Rufus in her arms. For a change, he didn't seem to mind that he was being cuddled and loved. "The dog stays with me," I joked and held my arms out for Rufus.

Keisha laughed again. "Of course, but he's just so cute. And warm." She relinquished Rufus to me and then dropped her arms to her side. "Thanks again. For the ride and for not leaving me stranded at the train station."

"Sure, yeah...it was nothing."

"Well, I'll see you around." She touched my arm and then stepped back. I waited as she wheeled her suitcase to the gate. Then, I loaded Rufus back in the car, and we drove off. I didn't want to see the reunion. I didn't want to see her get her hopes dashed.

2

AFTER MIDNIGHT

Without Ellie, the house felt empty and quiet. Almost too quiet. Ellie talked nonstop, and I'd gotten used to her constant chatter—about Boston neighbors I barely remembered, TV shows she thought I should watch, songs she liked, you name it. Sometimes, she even tried to talk about April and the kids. I drew the line there. I didn't want to bring them here. Not yet. I already saw them everywhere, even when I knew it wasn't possible.

Like now.

I thought I saw Audrey sitting at the kitchen table, her head resting on her arm as she watched me fill Rufus's water bowl. My chest went tight at the sight of her. My baby. My youngest girl. I could still hear her voice, in my head, asking so many questions, *Daddy, when can we get a kitten? Daddy, why didn't you go to Harvard with Mommy? Do you think I'll be pretty like Caitlin when I grow up?*

When she was still with me, her endless questions used to

drive me crazy. I wish I'd never yelled at her when she broke a glass. I wish I'd never said, "Give it a rest now, Auds."

I wished I'd listened more.

I wished I'd never lost my baby girl.

If she were sitting at the kitchen table, I would have pulled out the chair facing hers, sat down, and stretched my fingers out to hers. She'd laugh and call me silly, and then she'd swat my fingers and tell me a funny story. My funny girl. She was always full of stories. And this time, I'd listen. I wouldn't let my worries about making ends meet, or whether it was time to take the car for inspection, or if this was the weekend we had to make the drive to Connecticut to see April's family distract me from giving my little girl the attention she deserved. I should have been home with them that night. I shouldn't have gone out with the guys from work.

I blinked and then she was gone. I whispered her name. Rufus trotted into the kitchen, looking around as if he expected to see Audrey too.

It was going to be one of those nights. I might have to go for a drive.

———

IT WAS ALREADY LATE BY THE TIME I HEADED INTO THE LIVING room. It was late when I'd dropped Ellie off. She'd taken the last train heading north, so it must have been around ten-thirty, maybe closing in on eleven, when I left the train station. Before we drove to the station, I treated her to dinner at a bistro on Cary Street. The first time I'd been was before on a blind date that had been more of a bad idea than anything else, but the food was good. I started dropping in more often when the silence at home became too much. I figured my kid sister deserved that her last meal in Richmond be one that she hadn't cooked herself.

Over plates of scallops and linguini, she'd tried to convince me to come to our cousin Jack's wedding in Worcester. "He'd love it if you were there," she said as she twirled linguini with her fork. "We all would."

"Maybe," was my reply. It was what I always said. I hadn't stepped foot in Massachusetts in five years. Not since the trial ended. Every time I thought of going back, the bitter taste of anger filled my mouth and throat. I didn't want to go back to the place that took my wife and kids from me. But I couldn't tell Ellie that. She believed the old saying that time healed all wounds. Of course, she did. No one had been stolen from her—not like for me. My whole life died in Boston. And going back...I couldn't see it happening, but I couldn't tell my kid sister that she was crazy for wanting me to visit. Everybody thought I'd get over it. But you never really get over someone murdering your family.

I tried to push it out of my mind. Thinking about April and the girls too much pulled me into a dark hole that was too hard to escape. It was why I didn't have any pictures of them on the mantel over the fireplace or on my nightstand. I didn't need reminders of them everywhere. Their ghosts were always with me.

Maybe, it was just the chill to the air that made me think of ghosts. Septembers in Richmond were usually warmer, but the rain seemed to have washed away the last vestiges of summer heat, and now the breeze cooled my skin and made me shiver. Rufus was already curled up on the sofa with his favorite blanket, a faded plaid affair I'd found in a thrift store near VCU's campus. I bought it to have in the car when Rufus was still a scrappy puppy. But keeping it in the car proved futile when

Rufus started dragging it into the house after every car ride. So much for me being the leader of the pack. What the hell. He was happy with the blanket.

I piled some wood and kindling in the hearth and got a fire going. It was a little early in the season, but with all the rain, the house felt damp and chilly. I needed to get rid of this awful pall. If the house felt warm, I wouldn't think about that night. It was raining then too. And soon, it would be the anniversary of losing them.

My beautiful girls. April. Caitlin and Audrey. *April...damn it, April, I miss you. I hate this life without you.*

I hate my life without you.

I went to the liquor cabinet and poured myself a glass of scotch, neat. No need to dilute it. I needed alcohol to numb me tonight. The first gulp burned going down. It always did. Then the smokiness dissipated, the warm undertones bloomed, and the liquid warmth spread through me, pushing the memories back a little and giving me a little peace of mind. I joined Rufus on the sofa and kicked off my shoes. They were a battered pair of leather loafers that had seen better days. I should get them re-soled. I should polish them. They're good quality leather. They'd last a lifetime if I took better care of them. It's what Ellie said. It's what April used to say.

April.

Baby, I still love you.

3

AN UNEXPECTED GUEST

I wasn't sure when I fell asleep. The fire had died down, and Rufus was at the door barking. I raked my fingers through my hair and tried to shake away the grogginess. Then the doorbell sounded. Was that what jarred me awake? Someone at the door? I wiped my mouth with the back of my hand and then stood on unsteady feet. Rufus was still barking, but it wasn't that grumpy "who the fuck are you" bark he used on strangers. This was more of his "get your ass off the sofa and come see who's at the door" bark. By the time I got to the hall, I could see he was practically wagging his entire body. Whoever it was, he was happy to see them. Fuck, what time is it?

I turned on the light in the vestibule and then I saw her clearly through the glass. It was the girl from the station. I unlocked the door and opened it. "Hey..."

"Hi..." She looked like she'd been crying. "Does the offer still stand?"

I nodded. "Come on in."

Rufus led the way, jumping and barking, turning himself in circles to make sure she was following.

"You okay?" I asked her.

She shook her head no. "The fucker has a girlfriend. He never told me about that."

I gestured at the couch. Keisha sat down heavily then lowered her head into her hands and started crying again. What was I supposed to do? I didn't know the right things to say. So, I asked her if she wanted something to drink.

"Did you know?" she asked suddenly. "Is that why you made the offer?"

"I suspected when you told me the address. I knew who you were talking about. I knew Alex was seeing someone."

"Why didn't you say anything then? Why'd you let me walk into that?"

"I thought you knew."

"I would have never left London if I'd known he was fucking someone else."

"Guys like him are always fucking someone else."

"I wish you'd told me."

"Would it have stopped you?"

She nodded then shook her head no again. "Shit...I'm sorry, this isn't your fault. I should have known better." When she lifted her head again, her eyes were red from so many tears shed. Her walnut-hued skin was wan, from exhaustion, jet lag, from frustration? She looked around as if realizing for the first time that she was in an unfamiliar place. "Did I interrupt you?"

"Interrupt me?"

"Maybe you were asleep? God, your wife is going to get the wrong idea. Sorry, I should just check into a hotel."

"I don't have a wife." Saying it aloud feels so wrong. I did have a wife. She was just no longer with me. It's just me and Rufus."

"In this big of a house?"

I nodded. "It's just the two of us." I sat down beside her on the sofa. She smelled faintly of sweat. It was not an unpleasant scent. Even though it was chilly outside, there was a faint sheen of perspiration on her bare arms and neck. "It's just been the two of us for a while now."

"You're divorced?"

"Widowed."

"Oh! I'm sorry."

"It's okay. It was a long time ago." Five years. Five fucking years of trying to figure out why my wife was killed. Why my daughters were taken away from me. "So, you want to tell me what happened?"

"It seems so stupid now."

"Just tell me."

"He's living with this woman called Jenna."

"Jenna Barrow?"

"I guess so. Alex didn't say what her last name was." She grimaced. "She's not even beautiful. I could accept it if he were fucking someone who was better looking than me. But she's...average."

Jenna Barrow was average. Average everything. She wasn't particularly smart. She wasn't especially lovely. She was one of those women who usually blends in the background. It was a wonder Alex ever even paid any attention to her. I'd seen her at Secco so many times, trying a little too hard, wearing too much makeup, smiling a little too brightly as if she thought her smile would be enough to keep someone like Alex interested. When I first moved back to Richmond, a mutual friend sent me on a blind date with Jenna. I wasn't ready to date, not then. My wounds were still too fresh. And there was something about Jenna that reminded me of April. It was probably just the blonde hair and the faint trace of a Bostonian accent that bedazzled me long enough to consider dating her. I needed someone to remind me of April. Then the mirage faded. And I knew I couldn't go through with it.

I still wanted my wife.

I didn't want a substitute.

I was still thinking about April when Keisha said, "Everything he told me in London was just complete and utter bullshit."

"What did he say in London?"

"He said he missed me. He said he was ready to commit and we could make it work this time. That was just two months ago. I told him I needed time to tie up loose ends. I couldn't leave London without giving notice or finding someone who could take over the lease on my apartment."

"Everyone around here has an Alex story," I said. Maybe I shouldn't have been telling her this. "He's been with a lot of women around here. Broken a few hearts, a few marriages."

"And I was stupid enough to fall for him."

"It happens."

"So, what happens now?"

"What do you mean?"

"Well, what should I do? I only came here for him."

"I don't know. I'm no expert on getting back on track. I am the worst person to ask for advice."

"Maybe I should just go to bed."

"It is late," I agreed. "Come on. I'll show you the cottage."

We walked through to the kitchen and then out the back door. The cottage was just behind the house, separated by a stone path. My dad would have said it was within spitting distance. I unlocked the door for her and showed her into the small dwelling. It was not much more than a large living/dining area downstairs with an old-fashioned bathroom and a small bedroom upstairs. I should have opened the windows earlier. It smelled closed-in, damp, and neglected. But the rooms were in perfect condition. She walked around, looking out the window at the view of the yard, running curious fingers over the wainscoting. "It's nice," she said. "It feels homey."

"Well, it's yours if you want it."

"How much?"

"How much what?"

"How much do you want for it?"

"I'm not selling it."

"I meant in rent. If I'm staying here, I need to pay something."

I shrugged. I didn't need any extra money. The mortgage was already paid in full. I hated to admit that the money from my wife's estate allowed me to do nothing. I worked when I felt like it. I didn't need anything. "Don't worry about money. Just take care of the place. Maybe walk Rufus now and then, and we'll call it even."

"I can't stay for free." She folded her arms across her chest and gave me a stubborn look that made me grin. "I'm not a charity case. I just need to work a few weeks and get a paycheck coming in."

"Have you got a job already lined up?"

"No, but I'll figure something out." She tossed her head back. "I'm resilient like that. Always have been."

"Good for you. Well, you can stay as long as you want. And...when you get that job lined up, just pay me however much you think this place is worth then."

"What if I think it's only worth fifty bucks a month?"

"Fine by me."

"You're crazy. You could get at least one or two thousand bucks a month for a place like this."

"It doesn't matter. Look, you want to stay here?"

"Yeah, I need a place to stay."

"Then it's yours, and you figure out how much you can afford to pay me or something like that. And then it's okay."

"I've got one more question, though."

"What now?"

"Have you got some towels I could borrow? I left everything like that behind in London."

"There should be some clean ones in the closet in the bedroom. My sister was just here, and she was on a guest towel buying spree."

"Thanks, Nick. For letting me stay here."

"Yeah, it's nothing."

"No, this *is* something. You don't even know me from Adam, and you're letting me live in your home. It means a lot to me."

"It's fine. Just...yeah, be nice to Rufus, and we're all right."

"Being nice to Rufus is easy," she said. "Being nice to everyone else is the problem."

We said good night. I wasn't sure what the protocol was here. Should I shake her hand? Should I just nod? She stepped in and gave me a brief hug then repeated good night to me. I went out onto the porch and then headed back to my house. The air was still damp, but the rain had subsided. Maybe it would be better weather tomorrow. I went inside and then made sure the fire in the hearth was out. Rufus watched me from under his bushy eyebrows. When he saw I was heading upstairs, he trotted behind me. I guess he was ready for a little shut-eye too.

I was halfway up the stairs when I realized her suitcase was still in the living room. I retraced my steps back down again and fetched it from its position by the vestibule door. Her baggage claim tags were still fastened to the handle. She must've come here directly from the airport. It looked like she'd arrived at BWI and then taken the train to Richmond. How long had she been traveling before I found her by the side of the road? And why had Alex just left her there? Why didn't he at least meet her as he'd promised her that he would? None of it added up. The whole story would come out sooner or later.

So, I took her suitcase to the back door and looked out the diamond-shaped window. The downstairs lights in the cottage were off, but the bedroom window was lit. I could have gone over and just opened the door with my key, but it felt wrong. So, I stood there, wondering if she was asleep or if she was lying in bed thinking about Alex. Or, if she was planning her next move. I just wanted to sleep. I left the suitcase by the door and then went back upstairs.

I'd figure something out tomorrow.

Everything would make sense then.

———

THE NEXT MORNING, I AWOKE TO AN UNFAMILIAR SOUND. SILENCE. Rufus wasn't in bed with me, snoring. His pungent morning dog breath wasn't blowing in my face. My whole body felt stiff. When I stretched, my body sounded like an old man's, creaking and popping. I was only thirty-eight. My body cracks and pops like my granddad's. I'd slept in my clothes again. If Ellie were here, she'd have given me hell about that. She'd say only drunks fell asleep fully clothed.

I wasn't a drunk.

I'd had too much to drink last night. Hell, sometimes I had

too much to drink every night. When I stopped dreaming about April and waking up to an empty house, maybe I'd stop needing so much whiskey to fall asleep.

Yeah, right.

I took a shower, got dressed, and went downstairs. Where the heck was Rufus? Usually, he was under my feet the moment I get out of bed. In the kitchen, his bowl was full of fresh dog food. Looked like he'd gotten fresh water too. Fresh coffee waited in the coffeemaker. And then I saw the Post-It note on my mug: *Rufus and I are taking a walk. And buying groceries. You had no milk or eggs. --Keisha*

Keisha...? Shit, forgot about her. I'd probably forgotten to lock the back door again. I glanced out into the pantry. She'd found her suitcase. It wasn't still propped by the backdoor.

I took my coffee black and then settled into one of the kitchen chairs. The newspaper was already on the table, so I didn't even have to go looking for it in the garden. Most mornings were a game of hide and seek. My delivery guy never threw the paper on my porch. Sometimes, I found it under the rose bushes in front of the house, sometimes on the lawn; a few times, I'd found the paper under layers of ivy. I don't know what I did to piss the guy off. I mean, I complained once because he was late delivering the paper—I didn't get it until it was nearly lunchtime, and by then, I'd already taken Rufus for a walk and bought a paper. But I had a right to complain about that, didn't I?

I was just getting ready to enjoy my cup of coffee when the doorbell rang. I pushed the cup aside and went to the door. Alex was standing there, arms crossed, and an irritated look on his face. I went out onto the porch and said, "Figured you'd come by sooner or later."

"What the fuck were you thinking dropping her off at my

place?" He didn't yell or raise his voice, but the edge to it alerted me that he'd rather beat the shit out of me than pretend we were having a civil conversation.

"What should I have done? Leave her at the station? Let her try to walk into town from Staples Mills Road?"

"You didn't need to get involved," Alex said through gritted teeth. "You could have just left it at that."

"Fucking hell, you invited her here and you don't even meet her at the train station?"

"And you had to do it? How do you even know her?"

"I don't know her! I was there dropping off my sister," I retorted. "She was soaking wet and waiting at a bus stop for a bus that was never going to come because you didn't show up."

How many of my neighbors were peeping out their windows, wondering why Alex Jennings was on my front porch? It wasn't as though he and I had ever been friends. Not since I'd first moved into my house on Grove Avenue and he invited himself over, claiming he wanted to make sure I felt welcome. It didn't take long for me to figure out he only came by to see if I was going to be any sort of competition.

But who was I? A shabby widower completely fucked over by too many deaths. He'd taken one look at me and known he didn't need to worry about me. He'd pretended he wanted to get to know me better, but he only came that one time. The next time I saw him, he acted as if he'd never seen me before. But I watched him fuck over so many of the women who moved into this neighborhood. I'll be damned if I was going to watch him fuck over Keisha, even if she'd come here just for him.

"I didn't tell her to come here, you know." He raked his fingers through his hair. I'd once overheard him say that he wore it long because he said it made him look rakish. I thought it made him look like an asshole who was trying too hard.

"That's not what I heard." I'd only meant to think it, not say it, but it was too late to take it back.

"Look, she got the wrong end of the stick." Alex was practically shouting now. I glanced at my neighbor.

"It must have been a wicked wrong end if she dropped everything in England to move back here to be with your ass."

"I didn't ask her to move here!"

"You must have said something to make her come." I glanced over his shoulder, past the hedges, and hoped Rufus would lead Keisha on an extended walk. "All I know is I found her, she needed help, and I've offered her a place to stay until she figures out what to do."

"She should go back to London."

"She came here for you, you bastard."

I didn't expect him to take a swing at me, but that was what he did. It made my jaw ring and nearly knocked me off my feet, but I recovered quickly enough to shove him hard enough that he fell backward. He landed on his ass, and before he could jump to his feet again, I launched on him and landed a couple of good punches of my own. Hitting him felt fan-fucking-tastic. I punched him hard on the jaw and pictured the asshole that shot my wife. I kept on punching him and pretended he was the bastard who killed my daughters. And I would have kept pummeling him if Keisha hadn't shown up and screamed, "What the fuck are you doing?!"

I scrambled off of Alex and tried to explain, but he launched into a story of how I attacked him for no reason. Rufus wasn't buying it. He growled at Alex and nipped at him, but Alex was milking it for all it's worth, trying to convince Keisha that I'd lost it, that he just came by to apologize. She went to Alex and then said, "I can't believe you even came to blows."

"What the hell are you doing here, Keisha?" Alex pulled himself up to his feet. A bruise was already forming on his jaw. Good. The bastard deserved it. I could only wonder how bad my bruise looks.

"I needed a place to stay, and Nick offered me his guest cottage." She thrust Rufus's leash at me and then grabbed Alex's arm. To him, she muttered, "Come with me." Then she looked at me. "I'm sorry about this."

"You're okay," I said. "But you tell him to stay off my porch. You want him in your place, fine. But not on my porch and not in my house." And then I took Rufus inside and forgot about the bag of groceries she was still holding. Fuck it. We could go to the Village Café or down to Shockoe Bottom for breakfast.

————

I KEPT MYSELF OCCUPIED. I DIDN'T WANT TO THINK ABOUT WHAT she was doing with Alex or if he was even still there with her. I closeted myself in the rarely used guest bathroom under the stairs and focused my attention on cleaning up my scraped, bleeding knuckles and the scratches on my cheek. I looked like hell. I was certain I'd have a black eye by tomorrow morning but, fuck, it felt good to sock that smug bastard.

I usually didn't keep much of anything other than extra toilet paper and liquid hand soap in this bathroom, but just before Ellie had come, I'd gone to Target and bought a ready-made first aid kit. She'd nagged me about it when she'd come to visit last summer. I washed my hands and rinsed away the blood and dirt from my scraped knuckles.

If April were still alive, she would have given me hell for letting an ass like Alex goad me into a fight. I could almost hear her voice, heavy with exasperation, chiding me, "*Why couldn't you just ignore him? What was the point of even letting him pull you into his bullshit?"*

What indeed? The more he disparaged Keisha, the more he rankled me. He didn't care about her. He'd convinced her to come here, yet he didn't give two flying fucks about her. He probably said what he needed to say to get her in bed again. I just hoped Keisha didn't let him crawl back into her life.

He'd already fucked with my sister's head a few summers ago, and it had taken Ellie a long time to get over how badly he'd screwed her over. I didn't want to see the same thing happen to Keisha. I still felt guilty that I hadn't done more to keep him away from Ellie. She'd wanted a night out, so I took her to Prosecco over on Cary Street. The last thing I'd expected was that she'd meet Alex or that he'd decide she was his next conquest. I tried to warn her, but she was convinced they'd made an emotional connection. She never brought him back to my house. They always hooked up at his place. Later, I found out that he was seeing three other women at the same time as he was stringing Ellie along.

I needed to call Ellie, to touch bases as we always did. I was supposed to have a session with my therapist—I hated going to my therapist, but it was the only way I was ever going to feel better. I couldn't keep pretending I was all right. I knew I needed to deal with my wife's death. My children's deaths. I kept thinking I'd gotten it all figured out, but then I'd wake up again and there'd be this gaping hole inside of me that ate away at me and reminded me that I had nothing. Nothing. Just me.

PART II

KEISHA - A SECOND CHANCE

4

COMFORT FOOD

"How long are you going to stay here with that asshole?" Alex fumed. A violent, purplish bruise was already blooming around his left eye.

I stood by the sink in my tiny bathroom, wringing out a washcloth. I went back into the bedroom and handed the cold, wet cloth to Alex. "Put this on your eye," I instructed.

"You can't stay here, Keisha."

"Actually, I can. I don't have anywhere else to go." I moved back to the other side of the bedroom and sat on the windowsill. He was sitting on the edge of my bed, cursing and shaking his head. His long legs seemed to take up so much space. He glared around, casting a critical eye at the room, even with his bruises becoming more apparent. "I did come here because of you. And now, you've got someone else."

"So, you move in with a complete stranger? You know this guy is a whack job, right? I heard he killed his wife."

"You're insane. He didn't kill his wife."

"How the hell would you know? You just met this guy last night at a fucking train station."

"His wife *died*, you idiot. And I wouldn't have had to take up with a stranger if you'd been there to meet me—like you promised you would."

Alex was mute. He sat there, staring at the floor as if the answer to all of his problems would magically appear. Knowing him, he was already plotting to concoct more lies about Nick.

When I first met him five years ago, I thought he was the most beautiful man in the world. We were in London. It was one of those unusually hot British summers that were more reminiscent of the Mediterranean than England. I remember being a little drunk on Pimm's and smoking too much pot in someone's garden. Everyone from the dance troupe had been invited to this very posh house for dinner al fresco and drinks. I think it was the principal dancer's house. She was married to a very posh guy from one of those ancient families that somehow managed to hang on to their money when everyone else was going broke. And that house was like something out of a costume drama, surrounded by rolling green hills and fragrant trees in bloom. I was laughing at something one of the other dancers said, something stupid and witty and sparkly, and then Alex appeared in the French doors leading out to the garden and said, "Now, someone sounds like they are having fun..."

I'd been planning on fucking the guy who kept refilling my drinks. He was cute in a squishy way, but there were no sparks. I just wanted the release, that languid, liquidy feel that streams through your body with a good, orgasmic fuck. That's what I was counting on. But then I saw Alex and I knew Squidgy would never make me come.

Back then, I thought Alex was so decisive and assertive. I liked that in men. I was never one of those women who could tolerate a weak, indecisive man. God forbid he was someone who had to consult his parents or his friends before he made even the most trivial decision. Men like that didn't last very long with me. And Squidgy...he was a commodities trader who made unwavering decisions by day, but while I was talking to him, he changed his opinion to suit mine or looked uncertain when I asked him something as simple as whether he was going to stay the entire weekend or just overnight.

Alex, conversely, radiated this irresistible confidence that was like a drug for me. With his Byronic curls and swagger, I was hooked. I should have known better. I'd met men like him in the past. Men whose sex appeal was too off the charts. Men who wore women down with their *hot-and-cold* and *will-they-or-won't-they-commit* routine.

He ran circles around me for months before we finally settled into what should have been a beautiful love affair, but that was more about me waiting for him. Waiting in cafés, in bars, in expensive restaurants. Waiting for him to apologize for standing me up too many times and then giving me pathetic excuses and the silent treatment for *his* transgressions.

He'd apologize with mind-blowing sex, but that shouldn't have been enough. I was stupid. Like a lot of other women, I put up with this bullshit. And I was even dumber because I gave him a second chance and he fucked me over on the very first day of it.

Now, he was sitting on the bed—*my* bed—like it was no big deal that he'd fucked me over in London...and he'd fucked me over here in Richmond and was telling me to go away when he was the one who'd told me to come here in the first place.

Why had I ever wanted him? Why did I ever talk myself into believing I loved him? Why did I even think that coming here was a good idea?

All my life I thought I could find the one guy—the one who'd make me feel complete, the one who'd make me feel like I was the most important person in his life. I'd never felt like that. I'd grown up in a small town in Pennsylvania where my family was one of the only black families. My dad worked all the time. So did my mom. And neither of them had much time to spend on making me feel special. To them, being special meant getting good grades and not causing any problems. It meant not really being seen. It meant getting a degree that would guarantee financial security. That was important to them. They didn't want me to struggle the way they had. They wanted me to have the sort of comfortable life they'd always dreamed of.

All I'd ever wanted to do was dance.

They tolerated my love of dance. They thought I'd grow out of it and do something practical. So, my going to Juilliard's dance division was not something that meant much to them. To them, classical ballet was pretty fluff, not something their youngest daughter should be setting her sights on. But I did, and it was what destroyed my knee and ended my career as a professional dancer of classical ballet. I could manage teaching dance, but I'd never be able to dance professionally again. And I missed it. And now, I had nothing. No teaching position, no man who would take care of me, and no permanent place to stay unless Nick was serious about my being able to have this place as long as I wanted.

And here was Alex, giving me shit about taking up Nick's offer and trying to bullshit me about Nick's past. *He* was part of the reason I was in this predicament.

"Why did you ask me to come here?" I leveled Alex with a cold, firm glare. "If you were already fucking someone else, why did you even ask me to give us a second chance?"

Alex wouldn't make eye contact with me. He wouldn't even give me an honest reply. "How could I say no to you?" was his retort—like I was the one begging him for another chance when he was the one who'd shown up at my door.

"I didn't ask you to come looking for me," I reminded him. "I didn't ask you to come to London and track me down. You did that all on your own."

"Look, how long are you going to stay?"

"You're unbelievable. Why do you even care? You obviously didn't care enough about me to tell me that you'd changed your mind and were with someone else," I retorted. "So, why do you care how long or why I stay? I mean, I may as well stick around here."

"But you can't!"

"I don't give two flying fucks about you and Jenna. I need a place to stay, and I don't have anywhere else to go."

"You could go back to London...or Pennsylvania," he suggested, as if it was the world's best idea when we both knew it wasn't.

"Fuck you, Alex. You and I both know I'm not going back there. I don't need you. I sure as hell don't need you trying to make life decisions for me. "

"So, you're just going to hang around with that fucker and hope I screw things up with Jenna?"

"I don't care what happens with the two of you. I'm going to get on with my life."

"You can't stay here, Keisha."

"I don't have anywhere else to go," I quipped. "You saw to that."

"Fine, just stay out my way," he sneered. "And don't you come anywhere near Jenna."

"Just fuck off, Alex."

"You heard me," he warned. "Don't come near us."

"I don't plan on hanging around either of you."

Inside I was fuming, and I wished I hadn't stopped Nick from punching him a few more times.

————

WHEN ALEX FINALLY LEFT, I STAYED IN THE GUEST COTTAGE FOR A while and tried to clear my head. I didn't know what to do. Stay? I didn't have a job, but at least I had a place to stay. Go? Yeah, but where? Some of the dancers who'd left London were back here in the States. I could go to San Francisco, but it would mean eating crow just to convince my old friends to forgive me. I wasn't sure if it was worth it. Especially since it was because of Alex and going to them now because of him would be so humiliating. How could I go to them and say, "Sorry, he made me look like a fool...again."

I went downstairs and looked out the window. I ought to go over to Nick's, see how he was doing. Maybe he was ready to kick me out because of Alex, but so far, he hadn't come by and said I wasn't welcomed anymore.

Then I saw the bag of groceries I'd dropped by the door when I'd come in with Alex. I was supposed to have been making breakfast for us, and now it was well past lunchtime. Outside, it was still one of those overcast days, but at least it wasn't raining anymore. Over at Nick's, the lights were out, but the downstairs windows were open. I went across the yard and opened the back door. I called out for Nick but there was no answer. I didn't feel comfortable going through the house when he wasn't here. I put the groceries in the refrigerator and then sat down at the kitchen table and waited. The morning's newspaper was spread across the oak table. I glanced through it, searching for the classifieds and the job listings. I finally found it at the end of the sports section. Not many jobs were available. Most were waitressing or temp jobs. I circled a few with the pencil I found on the kitchen counter. I could call around and see if I could get something going. I didn't have much money in my bank account. My airline ticket had taken up a big chunk of the money I'd earned as a dance instructor in London, and I didn't have much of the settlement money from when I'd blown out my knee. I'd had to use a good portion of the money the dance troupe had paid to buy out my contract to pay my rent and my medical bills. It wasn't the most ideal situation. I had around fifteen hundred dollars left, which wouldn't last long if I didn't find something to see me through.

I didn't want to be a waitress again, but I probably had no choice.

I was still sitting there when Nick came in with Rufus. Before he could even broach the subject of my leaving, I asked, "Is Prosecco a good place to work?"

He shook his head and slid into the chair facing mine. So far, he only had one bruise on his face, just across the bridge of his already slightly crooked nose, but another possible bruise was blooming on his cheek. He raked his fingers through his wavy hair. "You don't want to work there," he finally said."

"Why not?"

"Alex goes there a lot." He rubbed his nose and closed his eyes. "And Jenna works there."

He rubbed his nose and closed his eyes. He looked exhausted and worn out.

"Are you okay?" I asked, pretending the news of Jenna working at the one restaurant that sounded like it could a cool place to work wasn't disappointing. Nick nodded and then leaned back in his chair. The light streaming through the windows fell across the tabletop. I felt guilty. He'd defended me. He'd been the one who'd taken me in, yet I'd gone and taken care of Alex. I should have been taking care of Nick.

"I'm sorry about Alex," I said.

"Don't worry about it." Nick shrugged. "He's been an ass since the first time I met him. I'm just sorry he fooled you. You don't seem like the kind of person who should ever have to put up with his bullshit."

"Well, for what it's worth, I wish I'd listened to my better judgment from the very first time I met him."

"Just...don't fall for his bullshit again, Keisha. He's no good."

"He said the same thing about you."

Nick laughed bitterly. "He doesn't know the first thing about me."

"He thinks he knows you inside out."

"Yeah, Alex thinks he knows about everyone. The whole neighborhood knows his exploits."

I hadn't expected the scoffing, indignant tone Nick directed at me. He probably thought I was ridiculous to be hung up on Alex. Was I hung up on him? I didn't want to be. Not anymore. But that was the crux of it, wasn't it? You didn't really get to choose who you fell in love with. The heart knows what the heart wants. But at that moment, when Nick finally made eye contact with me, something pulled hot and tight inside my chest and that old familiar feeling—the realization that this person is connecting with me and is seeing something worth protecting in me—made me look at Nick differently.

What if he was really the reason I'd come here?

My mom—ever the practical woman—used to say God had reasons for helping you make certain choices. Maybe I thought I'd come here for Alex and a second chance with him, but God thought I needed to cross paths with Nick. He seemed like a nice enough person. He took good care of Rufus. I never met a person who made sure his dog had food in the house but didn't care if he had food for himself. And he wasn't bad-looking. If I were completely honest, I would admit he was even better looking than Alex. He was as scruffy as Rufus, though. He would probably clean up well, but he needed some taking care of. His caramel-colored hair needed a good cut. Right now, he looked more like the sort of guy who'd wander the woods and avoid people. In a way, that's what he was doing. Except, he wasn't in the woods.

"What do you mean...his exploits?" I said, just to distract myself from thinking too much about Nick's potential charms. I couldn't think this way about him. I didn't believe in God. Didn't believe in some invisible figure guiding me anywhere. I made my own stupid choices. I was good at that without any divine intervention.

Nick stood up and went to the sink. He took a glass from the cupboard and then filled it with water. "Your boyfriend has a habit of fucking every woman who willingly spreads her legs. He's worked his way through pretty much the entire Museum District."

"You're just making this up..." But I knew he wasn't. Alex was a goddamned fuckboy. It was what had broken us up in London. It would have broken us up here even now.

"Since I moved back to Richmond and bought this place, I've seen him jump from one woman to the next. Single, married...he doesn't care." Scorn and disgust tinged his voice. "I watched him once. I was in Prosecco with my sister, and he came in. I didn't want to be there, but Ellie wanted a night out."

"Did he hit on your sister?"

Nick nodded. "He was relentless, and he weaseled his way into her life for a while. Did the whole 'you're so gorgeous, wow

we have so much in common' routine, and she fell for it. Just
like so many other women I've seen. He had her so wrapped up,
he even went up to Boston to spend a weekend with her. And
then he dumped her. And now when he sees her, he pretends
he doesn't remember her name."

"You should have stopped her."

"You think I didn't try?" he retorted hotly. "Your ex-
boyfriend is bad news, Keisha. You're better off without him."

"I know…"

"But if you're still thinking of getting back together with
him, you can't bring him here. I don't want him in my house or
in the guest cottage."

"Okay."

"I mean it. He's already caused enough problems, and I
don't want him hanging around if my sister comes for another
visit."

"I said okay." I glanced away, unable to look at him, knowing
that Alex would still think he could have his way. "I think I've
had my share of Alex."

"Good."

Just then, Rufus trotted in, his claws clacking on the hard-
wood floor. He hopped into Nick's lap and licked his nose. Nick
smiled for maybe the first time all day. "Hey, little guy…"

"Alex tried to convince me that you killed your wife."

Nick remained completely still. He flinched at first then
buried his nose in Rufus's rough fur. "He said I killed my wife?"

"I know you didn't. But that's what he's saying."

"I didn't kill my wife."

"I…"

"I didn't kill my wife." He said again. "My wife was
murdered. So were my daughters."

"I'm sorry. I shouldn't have even mentioned it."

"These kids, they robbed my house and my wife and daughters walked in on it...and they killed them."

"Oh my god..."

"So, the next time that asshole says I killed my wife, you tell him what happened."

"I'm sorry..."

"Jesus, is he telling other people I murdered my wife?"

"I honestly don't know. He blurted it out today to convince me not to stay here."

"I loved my wife. I still love my wife even after everything that happened."

We sat in silence. Shame burned inside me. I should have never told him what Alex said. It would not make things better. I guess I just wanted to reassure him that my ex was a jerk. But now, I was the one who felt like a first-class jerk. When I looked down, my hands were shaking. I balled them into fists and pressed them into my thighs.

"I moved back here because of what happened," Nick finally said. "I didn't want to tell anyone about it, but somehow, it all came out anyway."

"Do you ever go back?"

"No. It's too hard." Nick was still holding Rufus. The little dog was licking his chin as his owner balanced him on his lap. "Ellie wants me to come home for Thanksgiving this year, but I don't know. I don't think I can handle it."

"I could go with you," I offered before I'd even thought it through. Maybe he'd never expect me to follow through on it. It was already the end of September. We still had two months until Thanksgiving. Maybe I wouldn't even still be here by then.

"Yeah, maybe." He set Rufus down on the floor then pushed back his chair. His t-shirt was ripped by the collar; tiny flecks of blood dotted the front of the shirt. "It's a ways off anyway."

I stood up too. It felt like we should be doing something. I was hungry. He probably was too since neither of us had had any breakfast or lunch.

"Let's go somewhere."

"Where?"

"Well, I'm hungry. Aren't you?"

He shrugged. "A little, I guess."

"So, what should we be eating? It's my first time here in Richmond."

He shrugged again. "Southern food."

"Go and change your shirt then...take me somewhere where I can have a proper southern meal."

"You're serious?"

"I'm starving. I haven't eaten since last night."

While Rufus watched us from the floor, Nick laughed, and then smiled, and said, "OK. I know where we should go."

And in that instant, when he seemed completely relaxed and the darkness lifted from him, I was ready to follow him wherever he'd go.

———

WE ENDED UP AT A DINER DOWN IN SHOCKOE SLIP, AN AREA IN southern Richmond that was full of Victorian-style brick buildings that had once been warehouses and shops but were now trendy bars and restaurants. The cobblestoned streets and alleys reminded me of the little neighborhood where I'd lived in London. The floodwall loomed above us as we parked.

"All of this used to be a canal," Nick explained as we walked toward a diner. "During the Civil War, this whole area was burned to the ground by retreating Confederate soldiers."

"Are you a history buff?"

"No," he said, "but I've had plenty of time to learn a lot about the city. I went to grad school here."

"I thought you were from Boston."

"I am. But I went to school here. Met my wife here too."

Nick pulled open the door and ushered me into the diner. It reminded me of something from a film with its paneled walls, old-fashioned jukebox, and retro Pepsi signs.

The waitresses here were all hipster girls with tattoos and body piercings. They all had amazing figures and wore tight t-shirts and shorts with Doc Martens or cutesy vintage dresses and Mary Janes that would have suited Mia Farrow or Julie Christie back in the 1960s.

Our waitress was petite and knew Nick by name. She gave me the once-over and then she asked him if he wanted his usual table. He nodded and then gestured at me. "This is Keisha, by the way. She's my tenant."

"Lucky you," she said between clicking her gum. "Nick's a great guy." Then she looked behind us. "No Rufus?"

Nick shook his head. "He's at home. Can't bring him everywhere."

"We could have snuck him in again," the waitress said as she led us to a table by the window. "He's such a cutie." I had the feeling she was talking more about Nick than his dog. He was good-looking. He had that little-boy-lost quality that was irresistible to a lot of women. But for him, it wasn't an act. He was lost. And this waitress—the name tag pinned on her prominent bosom read Janine—was interested in Nick. She smiled at him as if he was a treat she wanted to gobble up.

"You having your usual?"

Nick nodded. "Bring her the same too. She's never had it."

"Don't I get to see a menu?" I asked.

"You said you wanted some southern food, right?"

"Well, yeah, I guess I did say that."

"Then trust me. You're going to like it."

"You will," Janine assured me. I don't think she cared if I liked it. All she cared about was pleasing Nick. "He knows a thing or two about southern food."

How strange was it that I was a black girl who'd grown up in Pennsylvania and knew nothing of her roots in the south? My parents never talked about their family trees past the relatives in Philadelphia and Pittsburgh. I'd grown up in Lancaster County, in Intercourse, PA, surrounded by Amish people in buggies and tourists who just wanted to gape at them. I was a small-town girl at heart who was good at faking being a big-city girl. I had to if I was going to survive in New York. It was the same in London. Fake the big-city girl attitude. Let everyone think I'd grown up in the projects since that was what they assumed of all the black and Latina girls. It was what they expected. If I told them I'd grown up with solidly middle-class parents in a house that actually had a white picket fence around it, they usually laughed or pretended to be shocked that someone like me had such a staid upbringing. My mother worked at a bank in downtown Lancaster—and downtown Lancaster was nothing compared to Pittsburgh or Philly or New York. It wasn't a big city in any respect. And to be black and live there because this was where my parents understood we could have a good life, was okay, as long as you thought this was the normal way to live. Being the only black girl in a class sometimes. Being surrounded by Amish farms and thinking nothing of how a horse and buggy could cause a traffic jam.

Once Janine disappeared with our orders, Nick asked me about how I could not know anything about southern food.

"My parents hated the south," I told him and sipped my water. "They didn't have any nostalgia for it. It was just this place that had ruined their relatives. That was what my dad used to say."

"So, you never ate southern food?"

"My mom was very into this idea of not being a stereotype," I said, remembering how my mother was the black mom who never made fried chicken when we had school picnics; who wouldn't let me wear my hair natural because she was afraid people would tease me for it. My parents forbade me to use slang and grimaced when I raised my voice too much.

"Did she ever make soul food for you?"

"I grew up around Amish people," I reminded him. "My mom was more likely to make German potato salad and roasted chicken than cornbread or spareribs. She only made soul food when my relatives came to visit from North Carolina or Maryland. Otherwise, we ate pretty standard, pretty bland food."

"Poor you," Nick grinned at me. "Well, you and I suffered from bad food childhood. My mom was the master of overcooked vegetables."

"Mine too!"

"And she thought all steak should be cooked so long it was gray and hard to chew."

"Oh God, my mom does that too."

We both laughed as we shared more childhood memories of strange food, of food fiascos, of our mothers' amazing ability to bake fantastic cakes and cookies, but they couldn't handle meat unless they cooked it until there was no moisture left in it.

We were still laughing about it when Janine returned with our orders—enormous plates of Belgian-style waffles and fried chicken. My stomach practically cooed in delight. I'd heard so much from the southern girls at Julliard about chicken and waffles. It was another one of the southern dishes my mother never prepared, but I always dreamed of having it.

Nick poured maple syrup all over his waffles and chicken. He flicked a glance at my plate. "Go on," he urged. "Pour some syrup on the chicken. Trust me."

So, I did as he said and he was right. It was better than good. It was divine. I didn't think I would be able to manage all of the food on my plate, but obviously, my hunger knew no bounds. I ate until my stomach nearly popped. The beautiful combination of sweet and savory was amazing.

"How did I go so long without ever having tried this?" I asked with a happy sigh.

"Yeah, well, depending on how long you decide you want to be in Richmond, I'll make sure you try some other delicacies of the south...but especially here in Virginia. You need to have Smithfield ham with some eggs, grits, and biscuits one morning."

"I can leave whenever you need the cottage back."

"I don't need it back," he said. "And I don't want you to leave."

"Are you sure?"

He nodded. "As long as you keep Alex away, we're fine."

"Okay. It's a deal."

"Then we're good."

And it was a relief to see him smile. It chased the ghosts and shadows away.

5

MIDNIGHT WALK

I was exhausted by the time we returned to the house on Grove Avenue. Nick looked pretty worn out too. We parked in front of the house and, before we left the car, he said, "I meant what I said, Keisha. You can have the carriage house as long as you need it."

"I appreciate it, Nick. I just need to get my bearings."

"I can ask around about jobs if you're serious about staying."

We sat there in the car, our hands on the upholstery of the seats, nothing separating us other than the cracked center console and the gearshift. My fingers flexed. If I inched them a little more to the left, I would be able to touch his fingers, explore the strength I knew his hands possessed. The air in the car took on a strange, uncomfortable tone. My fingers twitched.

Nick reacted first. He moved his arm and rested it on the steering wheel. "We had a good day, didn't we?"

"We did," I agreed. I released my seat belt and angled my

body toward Nick's. "Maybe tomorrow you could show me around the city, help me get my bearings?"

"Yeah, I could do that." He peered at me and smiled shyly. "You need to learn the nooks and crannies of the town."

Silence settled over us again. I resisted the urge to reach out and tuck a wavy lock of hair behind his ear. Nick let out a sigh and then he pressed the button to unlatch his seatbelt. The strap had rubbed the side of his neck and irritated his skin. I wanted to kiss him there. I wanted to smell his skin and see if his scent would attract me.

Maybe he sensed it, the possibility that we could cross a line. He opened the car door first. "We should go in." Then he got out of the car and strode toward the house.

I followed him. I didn't know if this was an invitation or if we were just going to say goodbye and part ways. His shoulders were slumped, his hands shoved into the front pockets of his jeans. I probably should have veered off and headed to the carriage house, but I followed his lead. I just wanted to be near him. I didn't want to be alone.

———

RUFUS GREETED US WITH HOPS AND BARKS. HE TROTTED AROUND Nick, nearly tripping him a few times, as we walked from the living room into the kitchen. "Calm down, Rufus, I'm going to fill your bowl."

While Nick took care of feeding the dog, I commandeered a corner of the sofa and slid my feet out of my Converses. In the kitchen, Nick hummed as he fixed Rufus's bowl. At one point, he talked to Rufus as if he expected an answer. The dog didn't disappoint. He made a noise that could have been canine speak, and it made me giggle. I could not picture Alex talking to a dog.

I couldn't picture Alex doing much of anything other than fucking. It was what he was good at. He was good at talking, too, as long as it got him in bed with someone. I wished I could erase him from my life. I thought about Nick and how he'd lost his wife and daughters.

What was I doing? Maybe all I wanted was someone who could erase Alex from my muscle memory, from my body and mind. Maybe Nick needed something like that too. But he still loved his wife. And of course, he would always love her. I wished I had the sort of friends I could call and ask for advice, but I'd lost so many of them to my carelessness, my inability to keep any ties permanent.

"You want something to drink?" Nick called from the kitchen.

"No, I'm okay." But I wasn't. I shivered a little, thinking of how Nick's wife's ghost might be in this house, watching over him. I wasn't even sure what she looked like, but I had an idea. Maybe she was one of those southern girls, petite and slim with a cute, turned-up nose and a syrupy accent. It would explain his obsession with southern food. But then again, we were in the South, even if this corner of Virginia felt more like the not-quite South. I knew its history. I knew it had been the capital of the Confederacy and there were still Confederate flags waving from houses and government buildings as if the South had succeeded in seceding from the North.

I didn't like thinking too much about the past. I think I'd inherited that from my parents and their aversion to anything that would remind them how so many white people still saw us as the evil other. Maybe Nick was like that--he thought I was nice enough, but he wouldn't want to kiss me, wouldn't want anything more than a careful distance with me.

I folded my arms around my legs and rocked a bit, closing

my eyes and trying not to overthink my predicament. Back in the US, with no dance career and nearly broke, unlucky in love again and looking for someone to save me. No, no one needed to save me. I just needed to feel loved.

When I opened my eyes, Nick was kneeling in front of me. Rufus was just behind him zigzagging and trying to see what was going on. "You okay?"

I nodded then thought the better of it and shook my head. "I'm not sure."

He braced his arms on either side of me. "Tell me what's wrong."

"I want to kiss you...And I know I shouldn't."

He looked surprised. Had it been so long since he'd thought of himself as anything other than a widower? As the man whose family was murdered? He looked down; I wanted him to look at me and tell me it was okay, but then I got tired of waiting, and I leaned forward and pressed my lips to his. His lips were surprisingly soft. And for a moment, he responded with a ferocity that told me it had been too long for him too. But then he pulled away, practically stumbled back, and pushed himself to his feet.

"I can't do this," he said. "My wife, April..." And then he lurched up the stairs and slammed a door. Rufus scrambled up the stairs after him.

It was too soon. And I felt like such a fool.

———

I ended up hiding in the carriage house for most of the evening. I couldn't bear looking over at the house and wondering if he was at a window, hoping I would just go away. But I was restless, so at around nine, I put on a thick cardigan over my dress, pulled on my sneakers again, and started heading west on Grove. I wasn't sure where I was going, but I figured I needed to be alone anyway. Maybe having Nick rescue me had blurred everything in my head.

So, I walked past the beautiful historic homes with their wide porches and seasonal flags, ignored the chill creeping in through my sweater, and let my legs carry me wherever they dared. After a while, I turned off Grove and followed an uneven sidewalk to Cary Street. I remembered this street name. There was a restaurant here that I'd considered applying for a waitressing position.

Prosecco...and there it was. Just on the other side of the street, its lights turned down to a mellow, intimate setting, its windows a little steamed. I crossed the street and glanced at the menu posted by the door. The fare sounded like typical gastropub nosh--crostini, pate, and cheeses as appetizers, the usual seasonal grub for mains with pheasant and venison taking center stage. When I peeked inside, most of the patrons were sipping wine and picking at snacks. And there, leaning against the bar and smiling up at a woman with bland brown hair and pasty skin was Alex.

Was she Jenna? The woman he'd chucked me over for? I thought about going in and causing a scene. It would be so amusing to watch his face crumple if I came in and announced I was his baby mama. I knew it was one of his biggest fears. But seeing him now, practically fucking this woman with his eyes when a month ago he was in London fucking me, infuriated me. I backed away from the window and crossed the street, heading away from Prosecco and not knowing where I was going. I just knew I didn't want to see him. I passed a vintage clothing shop and a toyshop with the most eclectic shop window I'd seen in a while. I stopped and pulled out my iPhone then snapped a picture of the sock monkeys having afternoon tea with tiny china cups. Couples streamed past me, some walking hand-in-hand, others with arms linked, but the sentiment from them all was the same--we are not alone; we have someone with whom to share our lives. And I smiled at them, without being able to begrudge them their happiness. I watched them as they peeked in shop windows, disappeared into restaurants, whispered in one another's ears.

No, there was no point in focusing on them, on being envious. I would sort myself out soon enough. My heart wasn't broken over Alex. I'd hoped for a second chance, but I'd known...I'd known when he didn't show up at the train station that he'd done a number on me. When Nick tried to warn me with his sudden offer of the carriage house, I should have listened. But I had decided if Alex was going to screw me over, I needed to be brave. I couldn't just skulk away with a stranger.

But now, I was living with that stranger, and I already felt more attracted to him than I should. My god, I kissed him, and I wanted more! What the hell was wrong with me? I needed to find a job. I needed to earn some money. I needed to find my own place and maybe put some distance between me and Alex...and me and Nick.

I huddled into my cardigan and kept walking into the chilly evening until I stopped in front of a restaurant with the charming name La Pêche. I ventured inside, anxious to escape the creeping chill. Who knew it could be so chilly at night in the South? I'd always believed that autumns and winters here were mild. The hostess was a tall black girl with a pixie cut that accentuated her sharp bone structure. Her full lips were painted a shade of red that reminded me of black cherries. "Table for one?" she asked as she reached for a menu.

"Actually, I just moved here to Richmond and was looking

for a job. I've worked as a waitress and hostess at a few restaurants in New York and London."

She gave me a slow once-over. "Do you have a resumé?"

"No, but I can email it to you or bring it by tomorrow."

She shrugged. "Either one is good. We're short-handed, and some of the people we've already interviewed were pretty hopeless."

"Who should I ask for?"

"Ask for Lorraine. She's the owner and the head chef," the hostess said. "She'll want to meet you...What's your name?"

"Keisha." Then, I took a chance. "I'm staying with Nick Reilly on Grove Avenue."

"Rufus's owner?"

"Yes, you know him?"

"Of course! He used to come here all the time. He and Lorraine, they know each other from the old days."

"I guess that works in my favor then."

"I'm Malia, by the way," she said and then handed me a business card. "Send your resumé here...Or come by tomorrow at around ten-thirty, before the lunchtime crowd starts arriving."

"Thanks," I said and shook her hand. "You are about to save my life."

———

I ENDED UP STAYING AND HAVING A STARTER AND A DRINK AT THE bar. I figured I ought to get a feel of the restaurant if I was going to apply for a job there. I assumed it would be a slow evening since it was Sunday. Sundays in London could be slow at restaurants unless you were in the West End by the theatres. I liked the elegant yet casual atmosphere of the place. The zinc counters, French-inspired menu, framed retro travel posters, and round marble café tables were intended to make you think of a dream version of Paris. It reminded me of a Parisian bistro where I'd once had a romantic meal with a French graphic designer who'd approached me after a performance. It was the sort of place that could make you forget the world outside, and when I heard French being spoken by the bar staff, I couldn't help smiling. It reminded me of my time in Europe. The two men were proper Parisians. Who knew how they'd ended up in Richmond? I could work here. I loved that the guests who came in were all ages--older couples dressed to the nines who were obviously out on date nights, twenty-something couples on first dates with that anxious, expectant look on their faces...young families from the neighborhood who wanted their children to know there was more to life than McDonald's and Checkers burgers.

There was a good vibe here. I finished off my French apple martini—and it was probably the best one I'd had since I left London, a true one—not with that awful green Schnapps in a neon shade. This martini had been prepared with smashed apple cider, cinnamon, and vanilla-infused vodka. I would have to remember this.

As I left, I thanked Malia again and then allowed a bubble of self-confidence to surround me.

I could get back on track. It wouldn't take very long.

6

MUSCLE MEMORY

I yawned as I let Rufus tug at the leash and pull me down the street. After a month in Richmond, I was starting to find my footing. I had a job, even if waitressing wasn't ideal. At least I had a paycheck now. Rufus and I fell into a routine. I took him out for a quick morning walk, picked up the morning paper on the way, and then, if I didn't have to work the morning shift, made breakfast for us.

When I worked the evening shift, Nick and Rufus were always waiting for me at closing time. We'd walk home together, sometimes talking, sometimes saying nothing. Nick made dinner, and we ate together, keeping each other company and talking about what had happened in the hours when we were apart. Sometimes, we didn't have to speak at all. We enjoyed the slow rhythm of our friendship.

Today, it was evident the seasons were changing. The hot, sticky scent of summer was already gone. Instead, the fresh morning air smelled crisp with autumn. My body protested at the air's chill and each jolt of my footfall on the pavement. I'd stretched before venturing out with Rufus, but my old injuries and stiff muscles didn't want to cooperate.

We'd just turned left on North Sheppard Street when strains of classical music caught my attention. I stopped, recognizing the melodies of Prokofiev's first suite from *Romeo and Juliet*. My heart began to sing with each note. Rufus, impatient to continue our walk, barked at me, his tail wagging. He danced back and forth, his claws clicking on the pavement.

"Just a sec, Rufus," I said and looked around. Where was the music coming from? I let Rufus lead me again. He seemed to want to follow the music as well. The more we walked, the clearer the music became.

It only took a few more minutes to find its origin. Just ahead of us, in the middle of the block, was a one-story brick building with a plate glass window. The door was open and inside were two dancers, practicing the scene in the first act of the ballet, when Romeo sees Juliet for the first time. I watched, mesmerized, as the graceful couple brought the courtship to life. My body longed to dance again. I mimicked each movement, wishing I were in the studio with them as my muscles remembered what to do. My knee twinged and groaned, reminding me that I was not as limber as I'd once been.

I wanted to dance again, even if it were only for myself. When Rufus tugged me again, I muttered a reluctant "okay, okay" and we continued along his usual morning route. I'd come back, though. I needed to reconnect with dancing, even if I could never be on stage again.

Usually, Nick was already in the kitchen when we returned from our walk. Today, he was still upstairs. I took advantage of his absence to quickly fill Rufus's food bowl and then headed out again.

———

FINDING THE DANCE STUDIO AGAIN WAS EASY. THEY WERE STILL practicing when I arrived. I didn't want to interrupt them, so I waited at the door and watched as he lifted her and the ease with which they moved. Most people claimed to hate ballet. They thought it stiff, old-fashioned, and boring. They didn't see the sensuality of it, the beauty of two bodies moving together, how the dance itself was a seduction.

I flexed my left foot, stretching it until it was en pointe. It felt good to try again after so many months. I'd tried before, but always thought I'd lost the will to challenge my body, to desire to lose myself in the music and let my body interpret a story. It had always been one of my favorite aspects of being a ballerina. I didn't need words to express myself. I could convey every emotion through movement.

As the music ended, the dancers briefly hugged one another and then came over to me. They were both slender, lithe, their bodies deceptively strong. They nodded at me and introduced themselves as Johannes and Olivia. He was taller than most of the male ballet dancers I'd worked with. His pale, sharp Nordic looks contrasted with Olivia's deep brown skin and petite frame.

"Are you here for the drop-in classes?" Olivia asked as she swept beads of sweat from her forehead. "They don't start until eleven."

I shook my head no. "I saw you practicing. I'm a dancer, or I used to be. And I wanted to start practicing again, even if I can no longer dance professionally."

"Welcome to the club." Johannes rubbed his palms along his thighs. "I'm recuperating from a knee injury. Olivia had back surgery last year."

"We used to dance with the Richmond Ballet," Olivia added. "But after the injuries, it was too difficult to compete with younger dancers, so we're both officially retired."

"I used to dance with a small company in London," I told them. "My partner dropped me—we both fell, and I ended up with the worse injury. Shattered knee, three operations...physiotherapy, and my career over."

As we compared notes, I began to feel a little of the old me returning. Johannes had come to Richmond via the Royal Ballet in Stockholm and a desire to prove himself on the American ballet scene. Olivia had grown up in Jackson Ward in Richmond and had dreamed of being a ballerina her entire life. I could relate. It had been my dream, too, growing up in Lancaster County.

I tried to read the energy between them—were they solely dance partners, or were they partners in life? Johannes always seemed to find an excuse to touch Olivia, and the way they looked at one another appeared to confirm that they were a couple. Maybe it didn't matter, but there was beauty in the way his hand cupped her shoulder, in the brief looks and smiles they exchanged.

"How much would it cost for a few hours a day to train?"

Johannes and Olivia shared a conspiratorial look, and then Olivia presented an offer to me: "We could either charge you seventy-five dollars per hour, which is the going rate...or you could pay nothing if you help us with some barre fitness classes we teach three times a week."

"I could do that," I said without hesitation. I'd led barre fitness courses in London as a fun way to earn money on the side. "I'd still want to pay, though."

"We can work something out," Johannes dismissed with a

wave of his hand. "It's always a pleasure to meet another dancer."

"We're usually here every morning at around seven-thirty," Olivia said. She was always in motion. Her expressive hands were never still. She also flexed and aligned her feet when standing, as though always subconsciously finding the best position to show off her dancer's form.

"You should join us tomorrow," Johannes suggested. "We like to have an hour or two on our own, but come by and we can stretch together, and then you can have the place to yourself for a while."

"I would love that," I said. I couldn't help myself—I hugged them both, not caring that they were still damp with sweat. Once we'd exchanged cell phone numbers, I let them return to their time alone in the studio.

Tomorrow, I could finally shake off some of the lethargy that had settled on me. I'd have to find my old leotards, my ballet slippers, pointe shoes, and footless tights. I'd also need my ratty wrap cardigan and leg warmers that I'd always liked layering when the rehearsal studios in London were too drafty.

I was going to dance again, even if it was only for me.

7

MENDING FENCES

By the time I managed to find my way back to the house, I'd figured out a good map of Carytown in my head. I didn't think I could get lost now, at least not in this section of the city. The only thing I had to do was avoid Alex and his new love. But a part of me was curious. I wanted to see what he was like with her. Then, a part of me wanted to warn her. Maybe she was as dumb as I'd been—thinking she could change him, reform him, with the strength of her love. I don't think anyone could change Alex. Maybe he was one of those people who needed to be taught an awful, painful lesson before he changed his ways.

One thing was certain: I didn't want to be the teacher of that lesson. Just thinking about him, about his smugness with Nick, his treatment of Nick's sister, and how he'd been with me, was the constant reminder I needed to stay out of his life. I didn't need a toxic man like him anymore. He'd burned me twice already. I refused to be burned a third time.

I was just opening the front gate when Nick came out on the

front porch with Rufus bounding ahead of him. Rufus barked a greeting at me and scrambled down the porch steps. Nick stayed where he was and lifted his hand in greeting.

"I was wondering where you were," he said. His shoulders were hunched, his hands shoved in his pockets. He looked for all the world like a little boy, waiting for someone to deliver a blow.

"I went for a walk," I told him. "And I think I might have a job lined up."

"Oh yeah? Where?"

"La Pêche Brasserie. Going back tomorrow to meet the owner, but the hostess seems to think I have a good shot." I bent down and let Rufus cover my face with smelly but wonderful licks. He planted his front paws on my knees as he stretched up to make sure I didn't miss any canine kisses.

"La Pêche, huh? It's a nice place."

"Yeah, Malia seemed to know all about you and Rufus." I pulled my cardigan a little tighter around me. "At least, she knew you as Rufus's owner."

"Everyone knows me as Rufus's owner," he said with a shrug. "I guess it's better than being known as an all-around jerk."

I picked up Rufus and cradled him in my arms. His warm body wriggled and squirmed. He nipped at my ears and reminded me there was more to life than just fucking and dancing.

Nick rocked on his heels. I could tell he was trying to figure out where we stood. I'd crossed a line. I'd kissed him and we barely knew one another. He wanted to broach the subject but didn't know how. Neither did I. I just kept thinking that if I had to do it all over again, I would choose to kiss him again and again.

"I was going to take Rufus for a walk..." he started.

"I can see that." I kissed the top of the dog's scruffy head. "I just came back from a walk."

"I was going to ask you if you wanted to join us, but maybe you're cold."

"It is a little chilly."

"Maybe you should go in and start a fire."

"There's no fireplace in the carriage house, so I guess I'll make do with a shower."

"You could go into my place and warm up by the fire," he suggested. He ducked his head again and then shrugged. "And when I come back, you can tell me how you ended up at La Pêche."

"You don't mind?"

He shook his head no. "It's nice having someone to come home to."

Rufus wriggled in my arms. He was definitely ready for his walk. I set him down on the grass and he scampered to the gate, barking at Nick as if to say, "C'mon, hurry up! I've got pee-mail to read."

Nick jogged down the porch steps and opened the gate. "See you in a little while," he said to me, and then he and Rufus headed off into the night.

I took his advice and went into the main house. The lights were on in the living room, but upstairs was dark. I hated dark houses. My parents' house was always dark. It creaked as though people were always walking across the floorboards. I climbed the stairs. I wanted to see how he lived. I wanted to know where he slept. I flicked on the light switch at the top of the stairs. The wide hall led off to five different doors, all of them closed. I tried the first one—it was a bedroom at the back of the house. It was empty and the air had a stale, dusty smell to it. The walls needed a fresh coat of paint, and the floors could do with a good sanding and refinishing. It was a good-sized room, and the bay windows looked out over the back lawn and the carriage house. Had he stood by these windows last night and wondered if I'd let Alex spend the night?

I retraced my steps out of the room and closed the door behind me. The next room was a small bedroom with twin beds. Framed photographs decorated the sage green walls. I stepped closer. The girls in the pictures had Nick's eyes and smile. Their hair was so blonde it was almost white. Both girls had a smattering of freckles across the bridge of their nose. These must be his daughters. My chest constricted as I examined each photo. They looked so happy, and the photos charted their short lives—from their birth until just before they were killed.

Poor Nick. He had to miss them like crazy every damn day.

The bedroom looked as though it were just waiting for the girls to come home. Not a speck of dust covered the white-painted dresser or bedside tables. Though the beds were only covered with woven bedspreads, they looked comfortable and welcoming, especially with the stuffed animal upon each bed— a rabbit on one, a puppy on the other. I felt like I an intruder in this room. I turned off the light and stepped out again, closing the door behind me.

The next doors revealed a bathroom and assumingly Nick's bedroom. It was spartanly furnished. A large wrought iron bed pushed up against a wall. A dog basket by the windows and a door leading out to the upper porch. A chest of drawers. A steamer trunk used as a bedside table. That was it. No television. No bookshelves. No framed photos in sight. The air in the room carried his scent, warm like nutmeg or pepper yet citrusy. He lived in this big house alone. He had Rufus, but I could imagine what he missed. Coming home to his family, sitting at the dinner table and listening to his daughters recount their days at school. I backed out of his bedroom, wondering how he could stay here alone. I hated being alone in big houses. It reminded me too much of how lonely I was. Better to be in pokey apartments with only enough space for one person. Then you didn't have to think about empty rooms that needed to be filled or missing people who'd never really been there.

You never had to think about being alone.

I left his private realm and retreated downstairs, but I left the upstairs hall light on.

It felt better being there when there wasn't so much darkness waiting at the top of the stairs.

———

WHEN HE AND RUFUS RETURNED FROM THEIR WALK, THE HOUSE seemed to come alive again. The shadows retreated and the ghosts of his past faded.

The fire had died down so he added more wood and revived it. I don't remember which of us decided that opening a bottle of red wine was a good idea, but we drank and talked, so much so that I felt drained. I asked myself why I wanted to hear his voice, that gravelly, raspy timbre of his with its faint Southern accent. He didn't have the thick accent I'd heard from so many men while I was on my walk. But he didn't really have a Boston accent either. I knew I had a slightly nasally Midatlantic coast accent. I'd accepted I would never be rid of it.

I was still pondering what to do when the telephone rang. Rufus jerked awake and scampered in the direction of the phone. Nick reluctantly stood and then excused himself. He lumbered into the kitchen, where the landline phone was mounted on the wall. I heard him answer and then say, "Hey, Ellie..."

I stretched my legs and then climbed onto the couch. The fire had died down a bit, but the room was almost too warm. I knew he was talking to his sister. I thought he needed some privacy. I went out the front door, leaving a curious Rufus peering up at me, and then crossed the garden to the carriage house.

After the warmth of the main house, the carriage house felt chilly and drafty. I went over to the steam radiator under the living room and twisted the dial to let more heat through. As I waited for the steam to pop and hiss through the pipes, somewhere in the carriage house my mobile phone tweeted. I searched the living room and kitchenette but nothing. I climbed the steep stairs and then found my phone, charging and plugged into the outlet beside the bed. I answered it without looking at the display.

"Are you alone?"

It was Alex. I should have known it would be him. "Yes, not that it's any of your concern."

"I was thinking I could come over. We could talk."

"No, you can't come here and we don't have anything left to talk about."

"I'm getting married."

"I don't care."

"You need to know that I'm moving on and you need to do the same."

"I am moving on."

"Then why are you still here?"

"I'm living my life," I responded. "I'm reclaiming my life. That's what I'm doing."

"Yeah, living with a drunk fuck-up that you barely know."

I pressed *end*. He'd call back. I knew he would, but now I knew better. I would check the display and then I would send him directly to voicemail.

I went into the bathroom and stared at my reflection in the mirror. I didn't think I was a beautiful woman, no matter how many men had called me that in the throes of sex or in trying to get me in bed. I knew my face was ordinary. I was not a stunner like Beyoncé or Halle Berry or Rihanna. I liked my lips. They were full, with that bee-stung look so many women tried to copy with collagen implants. And even though I was toned and sinewy from so many years of dancing, my breasts were still full, round, and firm. They were what Alex had liked best about me. He once wrote a poem about them that was published in *the New Yorker* a few years ago. He knew how to get a girl hooked—the lines of Shakespeare he could remember, the poems he'd write as odes to various body parts he loved so much. Remembering it now made me feel like a stupid schoolgirl. I should have known better. I should have been able to see through his bullshit. But here I was, an ordinary-looking woman with wide brown eyes and full lips, with a nose that was very straight yet broad, and hair that was just a mess of frizzy curls. I wasn't really looking my best. And if I would follow through with the interview tomorrow, I'd need to put on my game face. I'd simply use some ballerina tricks—makeup and a sleek bun.

I stuck my tongue out at my reflection and then left the bathroom. Maybe I should just go to bed. I went downstairs, thinking a cup of coffee would be nice when I heard tapping on my front door. I froze. Please don't let it be Alex. I didn't want any problems with Nick because of Alex coming around.

I went to the door and called out, "Who is it?"

"It's me. Nick."

I sighed in relief and opened the door. "What are you doing here?"

"You left..."

"You were on the phone with your sister, so I thought I'd give you some privacy."

"She just wanted to talk about Thanksgiving again." Nick looked around. "Come back over. I'll start the fire again. It's chilly in here."

I thought about going to bed. I would rather sit with him. I nodded and went back to the house with him.

In the living room, Rufus had commandeered a corner of the sofa and resumed snoring. Nick set to starting the fire again while I took some of the pillows from the sofa and arranged them on the floor. Then I grabbed the chenille blanket he'd draped across a chair and added it to the little nest I was making.

I lay back and then kicked off my flip-flops. Nick came and settled down beside me. Our arms touched. I glanced at him. He was staring into the fire. His jaw was tight.

"What did your sister say?"

"She told my family I was coming home for Thanksgiving," he said. "I told her I'd think about it. I never said I would come."

"She wants you there," I surmised, "so she told them and figured you'd give in to family pressure. It's an old trick we usually learn from our mothers. She means well."

"She does. She misses you."

"I can't do this alone," he said. "I've tried driving up there before...I just turn back around and then everyone is angry. It's...the memories."

"Where does your sister live? Is it the same neighborhood where you lived with April and the girls?"

He shook his head. "She's moved from South Boston to Worchester."

"She's right, though...you need to exorcise the ghosts. Make new memories there, close that chapter."

"I know. I need to find a way to even be able to go visit my wife and daughters' graves. I can't even do that."

"I could help you."

"What do you mean?"

"I could go with you and then you wouldn't be alone."

He glanced at me. I had to stop myself from reaching out and running my fingers along his stubbly chin and cheek. Instead, I lay back on the pillows and pulled the chenille blanket around me.

"We could either drive up together or take the train...whatever you want. We can stay at your sister's place or in a hotel. We can pretend I'm your girlfriend, that way they'll lay off you a bit."

He nodded. "You'd do that?"

"As long as Rufus comes along and chaperones us."

Nick laughed. "Where I go, he goes."

"We'll be the perfect trio," I assured him. "We practically are already."

Nick laughed again. "I like the sound of that."

So did I.

8

RETURNING THE FAVOR

"You've been working like crazy," Iris observed. "Time for you to sit down and eat something."

I looked up from the list of dishes I'd been adding to the daily specials placard we'd set up soon. All of the guests I'd been taking care of were either tucking into their desserts or had already settled their bills. I sat down at the far end of the bar and was about to ask what was available for the employee dinners when Iris set a bowl of asparagus risotto before me.

My stomach flipped for joy. I hadn't had time to eat breakfast, and I'd been running on empty all day, grabbing fruit and celery sticks from the employee snack tray whenever I rushed in and out of the kitchen with customers' orders. Javier, the bartender, set a glass of Chablis in front of me. He shrugged with his usual Gallic insouciance. "You can't enjoy risotto without a glass of white wine." Then he winked and headed off to the other end of the bar to fill a drink order. From the speakers, Carla Bruni's soft, sensuous voice crooned songs of love, casting a lovely mood over the restaurant and infusing the diaphanous cloud of conversations hovering in the air. My shift had started at ten in the morning, and now we were well into the dinner shift. My feet were killing me. When my shift was over, I'd gingerly walk home and soak them in warm water and Epsom salt.

I sampled the risotto and let the flavors wow me. Risotto was pure comfort food, and it was something I'd learned to appreciate when I moved to London and dated men who didn't mind lavishing a girl with dinner and wine before sex. I'd been too poor during my New York and Chicago days to enjoy fine dining, and the men I'd known then hadn't been interested in the dinner portion of dates. Besides, being a dancer meant staying as tiny and as strong as possible. I'd constantly had to watch my weight so that I wouldn't be too heavy for my partner to lift. Most days, I still ate the usual egg white omelet for breakfast and mixed greens salad and salmon or chicken for lunch and dinner, though I still allowed myself the occasional southern brunches Nick liked. Iris and Javier often teased me for my spartan eating habits. They tried to tempt me to sample more sumptuous dishes and risotto definitely worked.

Javier returned to my end of the bar. He refilled my glass before I could protest. "Your shift is over now, so relax," he said and then poured some for himself. "And so is mine. I only wait now for Sebastian to come."

"He should be here soon," I said in between bites. "He's always on time."

"*Oui*, this is true. But now—I must ask you. How in the world did you succeed in moving in with the luscious Nicholas?"

"Sorry?"

"Everyone here has a story, so we want to hear your story."

By this point, Malia and Iris were at the bar as well.

"There is no story of us if that's what you mean." I didn't know anymore how to tell my tale. There was no me and Nick, no matter how many fantasies they all conceived. There were moments when even I wished there was more to us, but it was too soon. And I wasn't sure how much of what had transpired with Alex I even wanted to share. They all knew him and Jenna. Richmond was a small town. "We're not a couple."

Malia raised her expertly plucked eyebrow. "So, he's still available?"

I nodded reluctantly. "As far as I can tell. I think Nick's still mourning his wife and kids."

"Such an awful story about what happened to them," Iris chimed. She swept her silvery bangs back and then cast her keen eye over the guests.

"Everyone heard about it," Malia added. "Well, we all heard Alex's version, which was so far from the truth, and then Nick's sister was here, and she set everyone straight."

"But how can you not be interested in Nick?" Javier mused. "He's so gorgeous with that crooked little smile and those dreamy eyes..."

Iris and Malia playfully teased Javier, reminding him he had a boyfriend and a David Gandy lookalike boyfriend at that, but he shrugged in that Gallic way and retorted, "A boy can still dream, can't he?"

"I, for one, don't know how you can stand living so close to him and not try to seduce him," Iris said. "Or are you running away from love?"

"I'm not running away from anything." My plate was empty now. I pushed it aside and looked over my shoulder to see if any new guests had arrived. "I actually came here to start over with someone."

"So, how did you end up at Nick's place?"

"The guy I was supposed to start over with started over with someone else."

"Ouch!" Javier covered his mouth. "So awful, *cherie!*"

"Was it someone Nick knew?"

I nodded. "It was Alex."

"Alex the poet?"

I nodded again. "If I'd known he would screw me over again, I would have never agreed to come to Richmond. I thought he'd changed. He convinced me he would never cheat on me again. And then I arrived..."

"And he was with Jenna," Malia finished for me. "God, he's scum. Good-looking but still scum."

The restaurant door opened, bringing with it a blast of cold air. Iris patted my shoulder. "You're off-duty now, darling. Sit down. Javier, she should have some dessert, don't you think?"

I relented and laughed. How long had it been since I'd had this sort of camaraderie? The last few months in London hadn't been the best, especially not after Alex made his reappearance. Too many people remembered the chaos he'd wrought on my life the first time around, and they'd thought I was a fool for giving him another chance. They were right.

"She looks like a girl who could use creme brulée," Javier said, tapping his index finger on his chin. "I will get one from the chef."

"But..." but there was no point in protesting. Javier, on a dessert mission, could not be stopped. He swished away, leaving Malia and me at the bar while Iris disappeared again to greet new guests.

"Have you heard the news?"

"Depends on which news you mean." I picked at my napkin.

"Alex is getting married in December. He came by this morning and dropped off an invitation for Iris."

"Good for him..." I didn't want to rehash the news about Alex's impending marriage. I'd always thought I'd be devastated if our relationship hit the rails. But instead of feeling like I was falling apart, I felt indifferent. And free. He'd already revealed his true colors to me. I still couldn't believe I'd ever been foolish enough to believe in him. And now, he was tying the knot with someone. How long before he screwed her over too?

"You're lucky, you know," Malia said. She took a sip of her glass of wine. "Imagine if it hadn't been raining or if Alex had actually shown up. Maybe you would have never met Nick."

Sometimes, I lay in my cozy bed in the carriage house and thanked my lucky stars he'd come along when he did. I'd often wondered what I would have done if I'd found myself truly abandoned. Maybe I would have slept on a bench inside the train station and then bought a ticket for the next train heading north. Maybe I would have found a cabbie who took credit cards and would have made it to Alex's on my own. But Nick found me. And I was grateful.

"I have to figure out a way to thank him for being such a good person, for helping me," I said, more to myself than to Malia. "I was thinking maybe I should give him a gift...or we could go to the beach for a weekend."

"The beach?" Malia looked surprised. "Honey, it's too cold for any reenactments of that *From Here to Eternity* kissing scene."

"Come on. Nick and I are just friends."

The door swung open again, and then a little bark startled me. I looked over my shoulder. Nick was standing there with Rufus on a leash, looking as grumpy as ever. Iris was already at his side, giving him an air kiss and bribing Rufus with a bit of chicken. Nick looked good. His hair was shorter now. He'd also shaved. His clothes were different—instead of his usual faded corduroys and shabby flannel shirt, he'd made an effort and wore newish-looking jeans and a dark blue fisherman's sweater. He looked like he was going on a date.

"Were you two supposed to do something after work?"

"No," I said. "Maybe he's meeting some friends?" He never mentioned any friends and none ever stopped by the house while I was there. I couldn't imagine him having a life barren of friends, even if the only time the phone rang it was telemarketers or his sister.

"Well, I'm nosy," Malia confessed, and off she went. She didn't so much as walk as shimmy in that sexy way that Marilyn Monroe had perfected and others imitated. The men in the restaurant picked up on it immediately. Their eyes followed her. Even Javier appreciated Malia's sexiness. He set down the creme brulée and said, "If I weren't gay, I'd be gaga over Malia. She's a little firecracker."

I watched as Malia made her way over to Nick, laid a proprietary hand on his shoulder, and leaned in to kiss his cheek though her aim was "off" and it landed on the side of his mouth. Rufus nuzzled Malia's hand. I tried to quell the ridiculous jealousy flaring inside me.

Nick and Rufus were mine—not Malia's.

What was I even thinking?

They didn't belong to me. Nick was still caught up in the memory of his wife. He wasn't ready for anyone new. Was he? And we were friends. We'd settled into that territory since I'd moved into his carriage house six weeks ago. I didn't like feeling unsettled, especially by misplaced jealousy. But as I sat there at the bar, my eyes were still trained on Nick and Malia and how Nick blushed and took a slight step back, but Malia was quick; she linked her arm through Nick's and laughed as she led him through the restaurant and over to the bar. By the time he was standing next to me, I was certain my knuckles were as close to white as they could get. I nodded curtly at him and took another spoonful of my dessert. Malia gave me a smug grin and then went back to the front of the restaurant.

"Hey..." he said as a greeting.

"Hi." I gulped down the coffee Javier had set before me. Why was I so angry? I knew Nick didn't belong to me. It didn't matter that we'd shared a drunken kiss. A kiss meant nothing. Not when there'd been no follow-up. "You're dressed up."

He shifted Rufus in his arms and glanced around. "I...I was going to ask you if you wanted to have dinner somewhere, but Iris says you've eaten already."

"Malia hasn't eaten," I quipped.

"Why are you telling me about Malia?"

"You seemed to like her."

"She's nice."

"Hmm. She is."

"Well, anyway, I was going to ask you if you wanted to go to dinner ...with me," Nick continued. "And I wanted to ask you if you could...help me."

The creme brulée finished, I thanked Javier and then slid from my barstool. "I'm done now, so we can have a drink some-where if you want."

"All right."

I avoided making eye contact with him. How stupid to wear my emotions on my sleeve, and Nick was so caught up in his world of grief that he barely noticed. "I'll go and get my things."

I rushed through the kitchen to the employee locker room where my belongings awaited me. I shook out my coat and then put it on, wound my cranberry red wool scarf around my neck, and then grabbed my handbag. I stopped in front of the mirror hanging on the door and appraised my reflection. I was not as beautiful as Malia. She looked as though she'd been carved from the finest dark wood. Her cheekbones were impossibly high and defined. Her lips were so full and sensual. I wasn't as lithe as Malia though I still had a dancer's body, thanks to training every day with Johannes and Olivia. I liked the tilt of my eyes that gave me a decidedly feline quality. Today I'd played it up with a little liquid eyeliner and had gone for a dramatic winged look. It suited the sleek ponytail I'd managed to tame my hair into, and the lipstick I'd chosen was smudge-proof, so my lips were still perfectly plum.

At least I'd tried to look a little Parisian today. I was working at a French-inspired restaurant after all. The slim-fitting black turtleneck sweater hugged my curves, showing off the slope of my breasts perfectly. And the ankle-length cigarette pants I'd found in a consignment shop on Ellwood Avenue made my legs look sleek and perfectly formed. Well, at least I looked better than the first time Nick saw me—every inch of me waterlogged and soaking wet. He was so used to seeing me without makeup and with my hair wild that it was nice to show him I could clean up well too. I buttoned up my coat, nodded at my reflection, and said to myself, "Away we go, my dear. Away we go!"

———

"YOU LOOK GREAT, BY THE WAY," NICK COMPLIMENTED AS WE walked down Cary Street. Earlier in the week, the Cary Street Business Organization had strung Christmas lights along the entire length of the street, from Virginia Commonwealth University's campus all the way to Nansemond Street, cutting through the late autumn darkness and reminding everyone that Christmas was eight weeks away.

"Thanks," I said and hid my smile. I rummaged through my pockets for my gloves, but they were missing in action. "I thought I should make an effort since I have a job now."

"How's it going? Working there, I mean."

"It's nice. I like everyone there so far." I tucked my hands into my sleeves and then crossed my arms. "Early days, of course, but they're very mellow."

Nick steered us past Prosecco. He didn't steal a glance inside. I shouldn't have, but I did and was treated to the sight of Alex, holding court at the bar. Jenna was beside him laughing. I looked away and picked up the pace.

"It's weird not having you around during the day," he admitted. He stopped to set Rufus down and let the feisty little dog lead the way. "I got so used to our lunches at the diner."

"You could always come by and have lunch at the restaurant."

"Would you be able to eat with me?"

"Only if we sit at the bar," I admitted. "But at least we could still have lunch together. By the way, where are we going?"

"What? Oh...here." He stopped again in front of a small restaurant I always passed on my way to the dance studio. I'd never gone inside, but it looked cozy and welcoming with its terracotta-painted walls and silver pine wreaths hanging in the window.

He held the door open and ushered me in. The waitress greeted us and called out, "I've got a wicker basket for Rufus. I'll bring it out in a sec. Make yourselves comfortable."

We hung up our coats while Rufus hopped up on the banquette. Nick shook his head at the dog. "You know you're not allowed on the furniture here, buddy. Down."

Rufus looked as if he was weighing his options. If he stayed on the banquette, he might be forced to wait outside in the cold. If he waited patiently on the floor, he'd probably get some treats *plus* a basket lined with wool blankets. He tilted his head to the side then hopped down and waited under the table.

The waitress returned with the promised items. She knelt, set the basket and bowl under the table, and greeted Rufus with a "Who's a good boy?" He thumped his tail on the floor, pretending he'd never been on the banquette.

"It's been a while, Nick," the waitress said, smiling hard at him. She ruffled his hair. "We were beginning to think you'd forgotten about us."

He blushed and ducked his head. "I've been busy, but things are getting better."

"Good! It's time. It's been a while." The waitress nodded at me. "I'm Meggy. Nick and I go way back."

"We studied at VCU together," Nick filled in. By now, we were both sitting across from one another on the banquette. His knee grazed mine as he adjusted in his chair.

Meggy suggested we have some mulled wine before we ordered. "It's damned cold out," she complained and then ruffled Nick's hair again before heading back to the bar.

"You know every waitress in town," I teased.

"Yeah, well...I did go to school here." He grinned at me. I was still taking in how handsome he looked with shorter hair. It suited him.

"I like your haircut."

"Thanks. I was getting kind of tired of the mountain man look."

When Meggy returned with our drinks, Nick ordered chicken and dumplings. Despite the risotto I'd eaten, I was still a little hungry, so I ordered a bowl of butternut squash soup. Once we were alone again, he launched into the reason for our "date".

"Were you serious when you said you'd go to Boston with me for Thanksgiving?" He sounded so nervous as he broached the subject. Color rose in his cheeks, and he kept his eyes cast down. He picked at his napkin. I wanted to reach across the table and still his hand, but seeing him like this was also charming.

I nodded. "I'll go. I said I would."

"I didn't want to assume," he said. "What about your family?"

"I don't do family holidays with them," I reminded him. It sounded harsher than I'd intended, but I hated the frustrating and unnecessary drama that always went along with visiting them. I'd avoided it so far, but I knew sooner or later that my parents would demand that I make an appearance, especially since I'd been back in the States for nearly two months now. "I'd rather go to Boston with you and Rufus."

"Thanks, Keisha." Relief swept over Nick's face. He smiled a little more easily now. "You're saving my life. You know that, don't you?"

I pretended to shrug it off as I sipped my mulled wine. He'd already saved me. I could return the favor.

PART III

NICK - A CHANGE IN THE AIR

9

GHOSTS

"Tell me about the woman living with you." Dr. Sheridan, my therapist, tapped on her tablet screen. We were in her Forest Hill office, sitting opposite one another in matching cream-colored armchairs. A grandfather clock ticked in the corner.

"Can we not record it today?" I asked. She always recorded our sessions. I knew she did, but today I wished she wouldn't.

"Any particular reason, Nicholas?" Dr. Sheridan never called me Nick. Just as I never called her Annabeth, even though she said we could be on a first-name basis. When I'd first told Ellie that I was going to start seeing a therapist for grief counseling, she thought I was lying. I guess I couldn't blame her. I'd been so adamant I didn't need it, but the longer I went without getting help, the more I felt like I was falling apart.

"It feels too soon." What did I even mean by that? It wasn't as though Keisha's living with me is a secret. We weren't even sharing the same space—she was in the carriage house; I was in the main house. But everyone assumed we were sleeping together, even though we hadn't crossed any lines...not really.

I guess I shouldn't have been surprised that she brought up Keisha. I'd bumped into Dr. Sheridan one night when I was waiting for Keisha to finish working. It was late, and I'd got in the habit of meeting her and walking home with her. Keisha had just come from behind the bar and hooked her arm with mine when Annabeth and her husband approached us. I'd introduced Keisha as my friend...and then stumbled over the words in my mouth and called her my tenant. But she was more than a tenant. And I think Dr. Sheridan understood it immediately.

"All right. We can wait, for now," Dr. Sheridan assented. "But I would like to hear more about her if you're fine with discussing her."

"I am." I stretched out my legs and tried to relax. "We're not living in the same house. She's renting the carriage house from me."

"How does that feel? Having someone living in such close quarters?"

"It's okay," I shrugged, but it was more than okay.

Keisha was growing on me. I liked knowing she was nearby, even if we weren't always in the same room or even in the same house. I could look out the window and see the lights on then know she was home.

"Nicholas, we've been through this before." Dr. Sheridan pressed her thin lips together and clasped her hands. "'Okay' is not a satisfactory answer. Please elaborate."

"Okay." I slouched forward and kept my head down. Christ, I hated it when she sounded like a schoolmarm, but I'd brought this on myself. I should have told her what she wanted to know from the start. "I like having Keisha there. So does Rufus. She's...good company."

"Rufus approves, does he?"

I glanced up and caught Dr. Sheridan smiling. "He lets her take him for walks. He doesn't even like when my sister Ellie takes him out, but he goes willingly with Keisha."

"I remember you once told me that Rufus didn't like most people." She picked up her tablet again and reviewed the notes she had in my case file. "Rufus seems to be very selective."

"He is. But he took to Keisha right away."

"How long has she been living with you?"

"It's been almost two months now, but—like I said—she lives in my carriage house," I explained. "We're not living together, not like that."

I'd gone over this so many times—with neighbors, with my family. It always came up in passing. During a lull in the conversation, someone would ask about my new friend—you could almost hear the quotation marks being set around the word. My elderly next-door neighbor had assumed Keisha was my girlfriend and, even when I told her otherwise, she'd gushed about how lovely it was that I had found love again.

"Yes, I know, Nicholas. She is renting your guesthouse. And the two of you have established a friendship."

"Exactly. Keisha and I are just friends."

"How did you meet?"

"Haven't I told you this?"

"No, I don't believe you have." She pretended to review her notes, but there wouldn't have been anything there. She recorded most of my sessions. She only took down notes when, for some reason, she wasn't recording us. "Some weeks ago, you did mention that you'd met and kissed someone. We also discussed the residual guilt you were dealing with as a result of it."

I shifted in my chair. Sometimes, Dr. Sheridan made me feel like I was a subject under the lens of a microscope. "I met her the same night I dropped my sister off at the train station. I gave her a ride into town. And when her living arrangements fell through, I offered her a place to stay."

She jotted down notes as she listened to my story. A part of me wondered if she was silently judging or praising me for such a random act of kindness.

"That was very generous of you, especially considering she was a stranger."

"Yeah, I guess it was."

"She never really felt like a stranger. Not after the first few minutes anyway."

"Interesting. So...would you say you felt connected to her from the beginning?"

"Connected?"

"Yes, as though you'd somehow always known her."

"A little, yeah. It was easy to be around her. It still is."

"What words would you use to describe her?"

I blurted out the first things that came to my head. "Kind. Sometimes, a little sad. Smart, pretty."

I could admit it to myself. Keisha was more than pretty. Sometimes, it hurt to look at her she was so beautiful. It was no wonder Alex had wanted her. The crazy thing was that she didn't even realize it. She was always comparing herself to Malia or the other women she worked with.

"I want to go back for a moment." Dr. Sheridan stood now. She'd set her tablet on the glass coffee table separating us. She smoothed down the front of her tweed skirt as she took a few steps to the window and adjusted the curtain.

"You once told me that your wife April would sometimes point out random women and say she could picture you dating them when she was gone."

I nodded at the memory. I'd always hated when April did that, but she'd liked the game, guessing who would be the new woman in my life. Since her death, there'd been no one. I didn't want anyone to replace her. Sometimes at night, I still felt like she was in bed beside me, her pinky linking with mine as we drifted to sleep.

"Would April have picked out Keisha for you?"

"No."

I knew the answer without even having to think about it. April never chose black or Latina women when she pointed out her hypothetical replacements. I'd asked her why once and she'd taken it as an affront or as if I were accusing her of being a racist. I didn't think my wife was racist. Maybe she assumed any woman I would be attracted to would remind me of her.

"She would have picked out a blonde. She usually did."

"Do you think April would approve now?"

"We're just friends. There's nothing to approve or disapprove of, Dr. Sheridan." If April were still alive, she would have been jealous. She would've made a smart comment about it to cover up her insecurities.

"Yes, I know, Nicholas. But this is the first time you've had a significant relationship with another woman since your wife passed away."

"And it's fine. Keisha and I are friends. Even if my wife were still alive, she would have nothing to disapprove of. We haven't done anything."

"Is that where you'd like this relationship to remain? As a friendship?"

"Why are you asking me about this?"

"Nicholas, you need to be honest and ask yourself why you feel so comfortable with Keisha. You spend every day with her. You're taking her to meet your family for Thanksgiving—that seems like more than a friendship."

"But we *are* friends. That's all we are."

"And yet you are going to pretend she's your girlfriend."

"It doesn't have anything to do romance, Dr. Sheridan." Now, I wished I'd never mentioned the proposition during our last session. "It's just so my family won't hassle me."

"You've kissed, though. You did tell me that." Dr. Sheridan crossed the room and went to a sideboard where a polished wood tea caddy, a set of pale white teacups, and an electric kettle waited on a marble tray. "Would you like a cup of tea before we continue?"

"No, I don't want tea." Whiskey would have been better, but it was still too early in the day for it. "Why are we talking about April and Keisha?"

"I'm aware that you're not comfortable with the direction of our session, Nicholas." Dr. Sheridan returned to her chair, now with her cup of tea. "But I do think this is a milestone for you. You've met someone with whom you connect. Someone you trust enough to have in your home and in your life."

"I get it."

"What do you think April would say to you if she could see and talk with you now?"

I tried so hard for so long not to think about that. April would have hated that I was still alone. She'd hate that I'd spent so long with only Rufus for company and that I hadn't bothered to connect with any of my neighbors. She'd wonder where my friends were and why I hadn't contacted any of the people we knew when we still lived in Richmond.

"I'd want her to tell me it wasn't my fault that she died," I said finally.

"Nicholas, it was not your fault. I know that you understand this."

"It doesn't matter how many times we talk about it, Dr. Sheridan." Everything inside me pulled tight as flashes of that night went through my mind. "If I'd been at home, do you honestly think those guys would have broken into my house?"

"Yes, I do." She raised her teacup to her lips. "I don't believe you would have been able to stop them."

"Maybe they would have changed their minds about invading my house."

In the three years I'd been coming to Dr. Sheridan, she had always kept physical contact to an absolute minimum. I appreciated that about her. She was more likely to push a box of tissues at you if you became emotional. She didn't try to embrace you or stroke your shoulder and provide anything that came across as insincere comfort.

She set down her teacup and waited for me to compose myself. I took a few breaths and exhaled, letting my heartbeat slow to normal.

"That's good, Nicholas. Take it slowly...one breath at a time."

Nodding, I squeezed my eyes shut and willed away any remaining visions of April. As much as I still loved her, I didn't want her in my head today.

"Would April be happy for you if she saw you and Rufus with Keisha?"

"I don't know."

"It's all right not to know."

"I want to think that she would be glad that someone was

looking out for me," I conceded as I allowed my eyes to open again.

"It's all right to move on, Nicholas," Dr. Sheridan reminded me. "It may sound trite, but there is truth to it. You are allowed to find new happiness. And there is no guilt or shame in doing so."

I wanted to believe her. Often, I did. Sitting here, as my therapist wrote down my thoughts as if they were lives worth saving, I could admit to myself that being around Keisha made me want things I probably didn't deserve. But at night, when it was just me and Rufus and my memories, the house seemed to breathe and sigh around me. When I could imagine my daughters playing upstairs or nearly hear the soft whisper of April's footsteps on the floor, it was hard to envision a life without ghosts.

———

IT WAS ALREADY GROWING DARK WHEN I CAME HOME FROM MY therapy session. For a change, there was a parking spot in front of the house. The universe must have been smiling on me. Some of the houses on my street were already decorated for Halloween. I guess it made sense. It was only ten days away. I didn't do anything special for the holiday. Not anymore.

Audrey and Caitlyn loved getting the house in Back Bay ready for Halloween. They'd pester April and me to buy pumpkins in different sizes that we'd carve into jack-o' lantern versions of us. We had a bright orange seasonal flag that April brought out every October and hung on the wall-mounted flagpole by our front door.

My parents had never really made a big deal out of Halloween. We didn't make jack o'lanterns or decorate the house for it. Our only Halloween decoration had been a cheap, plastic pumpkin-shaped pail that my mom filled with candy for trick-or-treaters. She'd turn on the porch light to let the neighborhood kids know that we were going to hand out candy. Once the pumpkin pail was empty, she turned off the light to keep any stragglers from ringing the doorbell. My dad used to grumble about the trick-or-treaters and call them mooches, but he never dared deny them candy. The last thing he wanted was to wake up to a toilet-papered house or dried egg splattered on the front porch and his station wagon.

Lamplight shone through the living room windows. The sight of it made me smile. Keisha must have turned them on before she went to work. She swore that Rufus didn't like the house being dark.

As soon as I walked through the front door, the mouthwatering aroma of roasted chicken tickled my senses. God, when was the last time anyone had cooked for me? Ellie, sure, but she was my kid sister. When had anyone else, though, cooked for me? Not since... yeah, it had been a long time.

I took my time removing my jacket and hanging it up before I wandered into the kitchen. Keisha was sitting at the table with my laptop, so focused that she hadn't even heard me come in. Rufus greeted me with a bark and then hopped from her lap and up into my arms.

"Hey, buddy." I let him lick my chin and cheeks. Sure, I'd stink of canine saliva, but this was unconditional love. "You helping Keisha?"

"More like he's been grabbing whatever scraps he can get," Keisha said without looking up from the screen. "I hope you don't mind—I think there are mice in the carriage house. Something chewed through the power cord to my laptop and my battery is dead."

"It's fine," I assured her. "I can check it out now if you want."

"Would you?" She looked up at me now and...yeah, I can admit it; there was something in her smile that made me want to move mountains for her.

"Yeah, no problem." I set Rufus down and ignore his grumbling as I headed for the back door and went back out into the chilly evening.

It was only a couple of steps over to the carriage house. I used the master key to go in and turned on the lights to the small downstairs living area. Nothing was out of place. It still looked as neat as it had been when I'd offered it to her. Everything looked the same, but her scent—that faint floral perfume of her skin—hung in the air. I tried to ignore it as I checked the seams of the floorboards, searching for entry points for mice, but nothing looked out of the ordinary.

Upstairs was much the same. Tidy, nothing out of place. I opened the closet and pushed aside some of the clothing. At the back, something glittered. Upon closer inspection, I realized it was the intricately decorated bodice of one of her ballet costumes. Keisha had told me she was a dancer in her previous life, but I'd never seen any real signs of it. The bodice was covered with tiny mother of pearl scales and scraps of tulle. Though it looked delicate, it felt heavy in my hands. I tried to imagine Keisha in it. I was so used to seeing her in her autumn layers of oversized sweaters and leggings. Imagining her in a ballet studio, her muscles straining as she held each position, her eyes closed as she memorized each movement... I could picture it so clearly in my mind.

Glitter dusted my skin as I continued to search the closet for signs of mouse entry. I came up empty-handed.

I was locking up when I saw the envelope poking out of her mailbox. I opened the mailbox and pulled it out. It was one of those thick, expensive-looking envelopes. Her name had been handwritten on the front with no return address. I tucked it under my arm and took it over to the house.

"Did you find any mice?"

"No, not a single one."

Rufus watched our exchange, and something in the tilt of his head made me wonder if he was the culprit. I nodded at him and told Keisha, "Our little buddy could be the mysterious chewer."

"You think Rufus did it?"

"He chews enough shoes. What's to stop him from chewing a power cord?"

I thought maybe she'd give him an angry look at least, but she only shook a finger at Rufus and called him silly.

"I'll pick up a new cord for you tomorrow," I promised her.

"You don't have to do that. It's okay."

"No, you shouldn't have to pay to replace it if Rufus is the culprit." I set the envelope on the table. "By the way, this was in your mailbox. Wasn't sure if it was important."

Keisha had risen from her chair and begun pulling dishes out of the cupboards so we could eat together. She put the plates on the countertop and then joined me at the table. She used a butterknife to slice open the envelope. The invitation she extracted was printed on linen finish cardstock. She held the card with her fingertips as though it were poisonous. She let it fall from her grasp.

"Class reunion?" I joked.

"No, worse. It's his wedding invitation."

"Whose? Alex?"

She nodded. "They're getting married. And he thinks I want to come."

"Will you go?"

"I don't know." She grimaced. "Maybe I should. At least then, I can finally close the chapter of my life that included him."

"I could go with you."

She eyed me curiously. "But you hate him."

"I like you, though. And it'll be good to close that chapter of your life." I didn't want her to have to go through it alone. We could be there for one another, just as we were now. "So, I'll be your date and we can show him that you're not pining for him."

"I like that plan. I'm definitely not pining for him. I'm pretty sure I'm over him."

"So, when is it?"

"In December. The weekend after Thanksgiving."

"We'll be back by then. Say yes and say plus one. And then afterward, we'll go out and celebrate that you're officially free of him."

"You're glittering." She brushed some glitter and sequins from my arm.

"It's from your costume."

"Ah! Yeah, the evidence of my previous life."

"Will you keep it?"

"It was too beautiful to toss out." She shrugged. "I worked too hard to get that part..." but she didn't finish that thought.

I didn't press her. I knew what it was like to have heavy memories. Maybe one day she'd tell me what she'd had to do to get that role...and if it had been worth it.

10

PRETTY BALLERINA

When Keisha wasn't around, the house was too quiet. I noticed it. So did Rufus. He had a routine now. He spent most evenings patrolling from one end of the house to the other, keeping an eye out for her. He'd hop on the kitchen chair closest to the window facing the carriage house looking for signs of her. If that watch proved fruitless, he'd jump back down to the floor and return to the living room where he'd prop himself up on the sofa and watch for her from the side and front windows. Each time his patrol didn't result in a Keisha sighting, he let out a canine sigh, growled and grumbled a little, and then retired to his favorite spot on the sofa with what sounded like a "harumph" of annoyance.

Lately, she hadn't been home much. She'd rush out early in the morning and, if I were awake, I'd hear the gate clang shut as she was leaving. At first, I remained in bed even when my curiosity was getting the better of me. Hell, she was an adult. She could do whatever she wanted, right?

She didn't need permission from me to do anything.

There weren't any strings attached to our friendship.

I just hoped she hadn't fallen off the Alex wagon and started seeing him again. If she was, they were playing a damn good game of hiding in plain sight. I hadn't seen him hanging around La Pêche. He hadn't been to the house, unless he was coming by when I was asleep or not at home. The only time I ever saw him was when Rufus and I were taking our evening walk and he'd be holding court at Prosecco, still acting as if he was over the moon with Jenna.

I knew she'd been taking extra hours at La Pêche. She'd mentioned it in passing one morning when we managed to have breakfast together.

"You saving up for something?" I asked over my cup of coffee.

"Yeah, well, no. More like trying to get back on track."

I asked her what she meant. I could admit it—I didn't want her to move, even if our living situation was only ever intended to be temporary. I enjoyed her company. Trying to imagine this house without her...it wasn't something I wanted to do.

Neither did Rufus.

———

THE SUN HAD SET. ALL MY NEIGHBORS HAD TURNED ON THEIR porch lamps or lit the candles in their jack o'lanterns. I still hadn't had the heart to do any decorating for Halloween, even though Keisha had tried to get me excited about it. I just couldn't. It had always been April and the girls' thing. Even if I sometimes thought that Halloween decorations were tacky, at least they added a little happiness to the neighborhood. We needed it. It was just a week until Halloween. Election Day would be upon us the following week. I was scared shitless by the turn the country was taking. I didn't like what I was seeing or hearing on TV and reading in the newspapers.

Whenever Ellie and I talked, she'd tell me about some new incident in our old neighborhood. What the hell was going on in America now? We had a clown running for president and a hell of a lot of intelligent people buying into his sky-is-falling schtick.

Ellie kept asking me to promise her that I was voting for Hillary Clinton, and I kept trying to assure her I was not voting for the clown. I don't know why she was afraid I would be the one who screwed up our chances of continuing in Obama's footsteps. I'd voted for Obama both times, and I wasn't one of those assholes who acted as if he'd personally disappointed me when we all knew that American politics wasn't easy.

I preferred the jack o'lanterns popping up over the Trump/Pence signs. When I took Rufus out, I let him piss on as many of those fucking signs as we could find. Tonight was probably a record. We'd passed six signs in one block, and Rufus had targeted every single one of them.

Maybe I'd been blind when I studied here. I never thought about Richmond being a conservative town, but I was a student, and the area around campus was so quirky and eclectic. Everyone that April and I knew back then had espoused the same liberal ideals that we had. It never occurred to either of us that we were surrounded by people who thought otherwise, even when Election Day rolled around. Most of the time we voted, and we didn't think much about it after that. We'd lived in that rosy-hued bubble of being in love and still not having the real world intruding on our lives.

Rufus tugged on the leash when I tried to keep following Grove Avenue. He jerked his scruffy head toward North Shep-

pard Street and pranced back and forth. It was his way of
saying, "This way, dude."

"Okay, Rufus. You're calling the shots." Maybe he'd sniffed
out a few more signs to soil. Sure enough, we found one that
was just right for his evening constitutional. Once he finished, I
pondered cleaning up after him and thought, Nah, fuck it.

"Good boy," I said and tossed him a treat as we continued
along North Sheppard Street. Rufus led the way; he knew
where he wanted to go, and I needed the walk. Everything Dr.
Sheridan had said during our last session was still doing
rounds in my mind. I knew she was right—that it was okay for
me to be happy, to move on with my life. But when so many
moments only brought home for me the absence of April and
the kids...I couldn't pretend I didn't miss them. Even when
things weren't always great with April and there were times
when the girls had bugged the hell out of me and I'd silently
wished I could return to the days of not being someone's dad.
No matter how normal it was to feel that way, it didn't stop the
guilt of not being there when they needed me from creeping
into my everyday life.

Every time I thought too much about Keisha, the guilt came
back. We were friends. I probably liked her too much; that was
the problem. That time we kissed... I didn't want to stop. I
wanted to be the guy who could kiss her and not have ghosts
watching from the shadows.

I was still lost in thought when Rufus came to an abrupt
stop in front of a one-story building. Warm light spilled
through its window onto the pavement. Rufus barked and wriggled, unable to contain his impatience for me to come and see
what he'd found.

"Rufus, why are we here? Dogs don't dance..." but I never
finished teasing him, not after I saw her.

Keisha...

I'd never seen her dance before, but here she was, clad in a leotard, tights, and toe shoes that nearly matched the rich brown of her skin. She moved so beautifully as if the music flowed through her veins and carried her along as if she was made of light, and dreams, and the air itself.

Everything seemed to slow around me. The sounds of evening traffic suddenly muffled. Even Rufus grew silent.

She wasn't alone in the studio. My neighbors Olivia and Johannes were there, watching from the sidelines. At one point, Johannes gestured for Keisha to stop. He came to her side and corrected the position of her upraised arm and, still holding her arm, led her through a movement so gentle it reminded me of autumn leaves drifting to the ground.

I could have stood there for hours watching them dance. Keisha was so concentrated on the flow and transition of each step. I'd noticed before how gracefully she moved, though she swore she was clumsy. Watching her now...the determination in her focus as she kept her eyes trained on Johannes and each change he led her through.

This had been her world before Alex stepped in. I could imagine her on the stage in London. So deceptively lithe yet curvaceous, projecting strength as she danced, as she slowly raised herself en pointe. The glistening sheen of sweat on her skin...I watched and wished I were the one holding her slender waist, that I could lift her and she'd know I'd catch her no matter what.

———

I'D NEVER BEEN A BIG FAN OF BALLET. THAT WAS MORE APRIL'S thing. In Boston, she and the girls often accompanied her parents to the symphony or the ballet. They'd get dressed up—Audrey always wanted to wear her favorite green velvet dress no matter what time of year it was, but April somehow convinced her to give other outfits a try. I should have loved it or at least developed an understanding of it. Both of my girls had taken ballet lessons through the children's program at Boston Ballet. April and I took turns taking them every Saturday morning. Like our house, their tuition at the dance school was paid for by April's parents.

"Ballet will give them such poise," April's mother enthused when I'd balked at the price. We'd all met for dinner one autumn at April's favorite bistro for boeuf bourguignon and coq au vin that we could have easily made at home. "Imagine how proud you'll be of their grace and beauty."

"Auds and Cait are great kids as they are. They don't need to put on a show for me to be proud of them," I started, but April set a censuring hand on mine and then she cut in with, "I've already enrolled them. I think they'll be darling in their leotards and tutus."

And they were.

I'd gone to enough of their creative dance lessons to love watching them find their joy in the music and the company of the other children. I'd swallowed the bitter pill of knowing how insanely expensive the classes were and that they'd been made possible by my in-laws because of the delighted squeals of my daughters whenever they put on dance performances for me.

Damn, I missed my girls.

When the house was too quiet, I could swear I heard them, chattering away in their bedroom, whispering secrets to one another. When I drifted to sleep, I felt them press goodnight kisses to my cheek.

Maybe they'd sent Keisha to me. A pretty ballerina from my

pretty ballerinas. I didn't believe in God or guardian angels, not even when I was a kid and my parents thought weekly Sunday service would cure me of my mischievous ways. But I did believe in ghosts. I'd seen my girls, seen and heard April so many times following their deaths to accept that there was no physical barrier between their world and mine. They watched over me. They spoke to me at night. Maybe they wanted me to continue living.

———

I COULDN'T SLEEP, THOUGH. NOT THAT NIGHT. I HEARD KEISHA when she came home. Rufus watched for her from his post at my bedroom window. From the happy little woof he let out, I knew he was pleased to see her. I got out of bed and joined him by the window. She passed below, a duffel bag slung over her shoulder. I thought she might look up. She sometimes did and waved to me before she continued to the carriage house, but tonight she kept walking. Maybe she was lost in thought.

Rufus trotted out of the bedroom. Knowing him, he'd use the pet door to go and visit her, then an hour or so later he'd return and resume keeping me company. But I stayed in my bedroom. As much as I wanted to reconnect with Keisha, I figured I needed to know what I wanted to say first. I turned off the lamp and lay in the darkness. My bed felt too big. There were no whispers tonight, no faint I love you lingering in my ears. When I finally closed my eyes, all I saw was Keisha, lost in the waves of music and dancing just for me.

———

THE NEXT MORNING, SHE LEFT EARLY AGAIN. THIS TIME SHE TOOK Rufus with her. Milky fog misted the air. I'd skipped the whiskey the night before. For the first time in a while, I didn't crave it. Once Rufus had returned from his nightly patrol, he'd hopped up on the bed and claimed his spot on the mattress. I'd woken briefly, patted his rough fur, and then fallen asleep to his canine snores.

Now my dog had temporarily abandoned me. I figured I might as well make myself presentable.

Keisha and I had a routine—we usually ate breakfast together on the days she didn't work the morning shift at La Pêche, but so many of her mornings she'd disappeared without a word, and her portion of breakfast ended up either in the trash or covered in aluminum foil and congealing on her plate. I'd been wondering if I'd said or done something to piss her off, but at least now, I knew the reason for her absence.

After I'd showered and changed into a relatively clean pair of jeans and a flannel shirt, I jogged downstairs and headed to the kitchen. She'd left a note for me stuck to my laptop on the kitchen table:

Rufus with me, back in an hour. Have breakfast with me. —K

I set the note on the table. It was almost nine o'clock. My stomach grumbled, reminding me I hadn't eaten anything more substantial than a ham sandwich for dinner last night. It would just have to wait a little longer. I set about making coffee. That would have to do until Keisha and Rufus returned.

She must have come in while I was sleeping last night. I'd left the kitchen in shambles. I hadn't washed dishes in days and there'd been a mound of crumbs on the table when I'd gone to bed. Now the crumbs had been swept away, the dishes washed, and the countertops wiped down. I would have cleaned up eventually, but yesterday I just never got around to it.

Keisha never mentioned the pockets of chaos that seemed to follow me. Maybe she thought it wasn't her business, or maybe she thought I liked it that way. April wasn't like that. She gave me hell about leaving plates of half-eaten food on the counter or slammed things around when she cleaned to make me feel guilty. Sometimes, it worked. More often than not, especially when the bad times set in for us, I scoffed at her attempts to make me be a man and clean up after myself. Damn it to hell, if I could take back all the times I'd told her to fuck off when she'd nagged me about it.

This would be one of those times when Dr. Sheridan would ask me what wishing to go back in time would solve. I could hear her calm, eerily neutral voice asking me, "What would it solve, Nicholas? Going back in time to right the wrongs? Is it simply for your sake or because you are honestly sorry?"

I didn't know the answer to that question. Maybe I just wished I wasn't such a fuck-up.

Fuck...

No, I wasn't going down that road today. I wasn't going to wallow in my grief, and guilt, and shame. I needed to move forward. Wasn't that what Caitlin said to me in my dreams? "Daddy, I want you to be happy... please. I get so sad that you're alone."

I had to get myself together.

While the coffeemaker gurgled, I figured I could at least do something to make the house a little more cheerful. When Ellie was here, she'd made a wreath of sage and autumn leaves to hang on the front door. She'd wanted to put it up immediately, but it had only been August and I thought she was jumping the gun. I'd stored it in the pantry, figuring it would come to use eventually.

Well, there was no time like the present. As soon as I

opened the door to the pantry, the fresh scent of sage filled my nostrils. Elle had wrapped it in an old bed sheet to keep it from getting dusty. I lifted the wreath and carried it through the kitchen and dining room to the front door. Once I'd hung it, I took a couple of steps back and folded my arms. It did look better with the wreath hanging there. It would probably look even better with more decorations, but the wreath was enough. It would probably make my neighbors happy.

Inside again, the warm scent of coffee greeted me. I sat down at the table, pulled my laptop over, and checked my email. Two new emails from Ellie—I could read those later, one from Dr. Sheridan's office—I opened that one. She'd sent me a reminder about booking times before Thanksgiving and Christmas rolled around and a list of questions to think about before our next session—the homework she assigned whenever we met. I printed them out and swore I'd review them this time, but most likely, I would never get around to it. I think I was a little afraid of the answers that would spew out of me. I wasn't even sure why I was scared of them, but I had the feeling that it would reveal something shitty and unlovable about me.

On a whim, I Googled Keisha's name. It sounded more stalk-erish than it was. I just wanted to find some videos of her dancing. She never talked about her pre-Richmond life, not since those first few nights. It was as if she turned the key and locked the door to her life in London. Maybe I wasn't asking the right questions. Or maybe I wasn't listening. But I think I was. She'd never said anything during our breakfasts or walks together that she was going to start dancing again. I would have remembered it.

The first page of hits featured links to Facebook pages for Julliard Dance alumni and the dance company she'd been part of in London. I scrolled down the list until I found the first video, clips from a performance called "Variations in Love." Clad in a flesh-toned leotard and toe shoes, she danced alone in the two-minute clip, moving so fluidly as though her entire body were synthesized of music.

Every inch of her body exuded strength as she dominated the floor with her routine. I could feel my pulse quickening as I watched the clip. Those two minutes could have gone on forever. She mesmerized me. My mouth went dry watching how she moved, how she seemed possessed by the music, and how the emotions her moves conveyed were so palpable.

I recognized the music accompanying her routine. It was "Babylon," a David Gray song that April and I had chosen as our first dance as a married couple. Had she chosen it herself or had the choreographer decided which pieces would best match each dance?

Once the clip ended, I returned to the Google list, finding more links now to photoshoots and articles, all from her time in London. One in particular, from *the Guardian*, singled out the season's Bright Young Things in Dance. I read the short profile that briefly covered her time in the US and highlighted how she'd impressed the artistic director and principal dancers of the London-based troupe she'd eventually joined. But what caught me was the image they'd chosen. Keisha was naked and reclining on a settee with only a pair of toe shoes and a wisp of strategically placed white tulle.

Oh, God. She was so beautiful. Her dark skin looked as though it had been honed from a perfect piece of rosewood. I took in the sight of her lithe limbs and the way the light spilled over the curve of her breasts. She was...

"Why are you Googling me?"

I scrambled to close my browser window and tried to play it

off as if I hadn't been staring at a nude picture of her. The words formed in my mouth but nothing sensible came out.

"Just ask me," she said, putting me out of my misery. "If you want to know something about me, if you want anything from me...just ask."

11

SECRETS

By Halloween, the last remnants of summer had finally given way to a chilly autumn. In the mornings, frost dusted the sidewalks and the days grew shorter. My neighbors had already begun stringing lights on their porch and deck railings in preparation for the heavy winter nights. I even gave in when Keisha asked about putting up lights.

In the five years I'd lived in the house, I'd done little more than make it somewhat livable. In the few months that Keisha and I had become friends, she had managed to soften some of the house's edges. One day, I came home and she'd hung deep blue velvet curtains in the living room. Another day, matching velvet throw pillows appeared on the couch and suddenly, a striped rug that seemed to glow with warm orange, yellow, and red on the floor appeared in my bedroom. I didn't ask where she found these things. I liked how she was trying to make a house into a home, even if she didn't live with me and neither of us knew how long she'd stay.

Somehow, she even convinced me to help her hand out

trick-or-treat candy. I'd just come home from a grief counseling session when she shoved a cowboy hat and boots at me.

"Put these on," she said and pushed me toward the kitchen. "The kids are already out in full force."

She'd already changed into her costume for the evening and transformed herself into the perfect music box ballerina in a pale pink leotard with matching tights, a tulle skirt, and soft ballet slippers. Rufus had it easy—Keisha tied a red bandana around his neck and informed him that he was a cowpoke for the evening. She'd even prepped with a little decoration: three jack o'lanterns formed a neat line to the front door and inside the house, fake spider webs hung from the pendant lamp, and three carved pumpkins were on display—and already set a huge glass fishbowl full of candy on the console table in the vestibule.

I didn't bother to fight it, even if I wasn't in the mood. Halloween always brought back too many memories, but I had to learn to deal with them. I couldn't stay in this bubble and pretend that the world stopped moving when I lost my wife and kids.

Keisha had bought what I thought would be way too many bags of candy to hand out to trick-or-treaters, but we ran out of it sooner than I thought possible. Some of the kids asked for selfies with us.

I tried to imagine what it would have been like, taking Auds and Cait around the neighborhood, watching them get their fill of candy, and collecting money for UNICEF. I could picture them in their favorite costumes–Auds in her princess outfit and Cait dressed as an old-school explorer from her favorite video game--swinging their pumpkin-shaped baskets and racing from house to house, screaming "trick or treat" and shrieking with delight each time they'd get full-sized candy bars.

Once word spread that we were out of candy, the rush died down. Keisha turned off the porch light and locked the front door while I brewed coffee for us.

"You look good as a cowboy," Keisha said as she joined me in the kitchen. She lifted the cowboy hat from my head and set it on hers. We were so close I felt the heat from her body meet mine.

"You make a beautiful ballerina." I leaned against the edge of the countertop. She stepped back and curtsied for me, dipping low and crossing her arms. As she rose, she wobbled a little. I went to steady her, but she waved me away. "It's just my knee. Same old, same old."

"Sorry..."

"Don't apologize, Nick." Keisha took off the hat now and set it on the table. "You're not the one who dropped me."

"Maybe you shouldn't push yourself so hard when you practice," I ventured.

We still hadn't talked about her dancing again. She sucked in her lower lip then pressed her lips together. She still disappeared in the early hours of the morning and returned sometimes, looking wilted but happy.

"What are you talking about?" Her voice sounded so faint.

"I saw you, Keisha. At the dance studio Olivia and Hannes run over on North Sheppard."

"I was going to tell you. I just wanted to feel like I could really do it again before I said anything."

I think I understood what she meant. Sometimes, when the silence was too great, I could almost feel my past coming to life around me. The forgotten conversations suddenly returning, the wisps of laughter, and the gentle touches reminding me of what I'd once had and would probably never have again. Not like it used to be.

"I missed it. Dancing, I mean. It's always been a part of me. And not dancing...it was like a part of me was gone."

"You were beautiful." I let the words take flight. I didn't want to hold them in. "You made me wish I could dance with you."

She looked up now, a sweet smile curving her lips. "Maybe you should come with me one morning. I'm pretty sure Johannes has a pair of tights you can borrow."

"I'll skip the tights," I laughed. "Maybe I'll just settle for watching you dance."

Behind me, the coffee machine's gurgling finally came to a stop. It hissed as the last drop of liquid dripped into the decanter.

"I'll dance for you whenever you want." She reached up and began unpinning her hair. I moved behind her to help. It felt so normal to do, to feel her hair between my fingers, for her fingertips to brush against mine. If I kissed her, would she push me away?

The longer I stood there, watching her uncoil her hair, the more I wished I could revisit that night when she dared to kiss me. I stepped away, trying to ignore the tightness pulling within me. I shoved her hairpins in the pocket of my jeans and told myself I'd return them later.

I focused on pouring coffee for us both. Keisha pulled out a chair and sat down at the table. The makeup she'd applied earlier was already fading. She rolled her shoulders and sighed. When she closed her eyes, I let myself take in the sight of her full lips and once again remember how she'd kissed me, how I'd nearly given in to the hunger to be kissed again, to be wanted and to want something so badly.

I joined her at the table with our mugs of coffee. Rufus wandered in from the living room, his curiosity most likely getting the better of him. He was probably hoping there were scraps of food waiting for him.

"I should have told you," she said suddenly, picking up the conversation again, "every time I left the house, I thought about telling you that I wanted to dance again, that I *am* dancing again...but I felt silly for wanting it so much."

"There's nothing wrong with wanting something, especially when it's been your passion."

"I know. And it's so silly...I can never dance professionally again. My body reminds me of that little fact all the time."

"Were you scared I'd laugh at you?"

"Maybe. Not many people in my life were very supportive of my dancing." Keisha cupped her hands around her mug of coffee. "Maybe I just needed to keep it a secret so it felt like it was just for me."

"Sometimes, it's okay to keep a secret for a while." But I knew it wasn't true even as I said it. Secrets were what ate away at my marriage.

Secrets never really did anyone any good, did they?

———

"WHAT IS WRONG WITH THIS FREAKING COUNTRY?" KEISHA lamented after downing another glass of red wine. We'd already emptied the first bottle of wine and uncorked a second bottle. Rufus eyed us from his position in the armchair by the front window. I sat on the other end of the couch, my shoulders slumped as the results began to pour in. How could this be happening? How could anyone believe that a man who thought nothing of making misogynistic comments, who encouraged people to use violence against anyone who didn't agree with him, and emboldened bigots and racists to harass immigrants and minorities and anyone who simply wasn't...white, would be a good leader for our country?

"I can't believe this..." I'd said the same thing so many times.

"I thought we were smarter than this." All the frustration in Keisha seemed to vibrate through her body. She couldn't sit still. Twice in the last few minutes, she'd jumped to her feet, paced the length of the living room, shaking her head all the while and muttering swearwords. "I kept telling everyone I knew in London that this clown would never be president."

"Were you there for the Brexit vote?"

She nodded. "Everyone I knew was so shocked. I don't think anyone believed that referendum would actually lead to Britain choosing to leave the European Union. Right after the vote, all these people who'd voted yes were claiming they had voter's remorse or that they didn't think their vote would count."

"Maybe it's the same here." I wanted to believe that we Americans weren't so naive, that we didn't honestly believe the rhetoric, and that more of us would come to our senses. But I'd lived here in Richmond, a city that still celebrated its role in the Civil War, too long.

Keisha's smirk let me know she wasn't convinced. She held out her glass. "Just pour me another one."

"Gladly." I filled her glass with more Grenache. By midnight, we'd polished off three bottles.

My brain almost hurt from trying to figure out what all of this would mean once the veneer of something new wore off. Would Americans wake up and realize what they'd done and have voter's remorse as Keisha swore so many Brits had?

All I knew was that I wished there was some way to turn back the clock, to prevent any of this from happening. The only thing I didn't want to erase was meeting Keisha. That rainy evening... I'd nearly driven past her. I drained my glass and set it down on the floor.

"I wish I could sleep through tomorrow," I muttered.

"It wouldn't help." Keisha reached for the chenille throw she'd claimed as her own. She draped it over her legs. "Sleep through tomorrow, wake up another day to the same reality."

"If we were Sleeping Beauty, we could wake up months or even years later to a new reality."

"Sorry, no princes or princesses kissing us."

I reached for the remote to turn down the volume, but Keisha beat me to it. Her index finger was already pressing the down button to tune out the bad news.

"I don't know how I will even sleep tonight." She said it so softly, like an afterthought that had taken on a life of its own. "It feels like we're at the brink of the end of the world. And there's no turning back."

I turned to watch her. Sometimes, she seemed to brim over with emotions. I'd been so used to being on my own, to cutting off everyone around me. It had just been Rufus and me for so long. Now, we were three.

"I don't want to sleep alone tonight. I don't think I'll sleep anyway." She clicked off the television, saving us from sinking further into our Election Day funk. Rufus lifted his head and then yawned and settled down again, closing his eyes and breathing deeply. Now that he'd claimed his armchair, he didn't seem very interested in leaving it.

"You can stay here." I didn't want to sleep alone either. I couldn't get my head around the sudden shift of my world. I tried to remind myself that this was temporary. Whatever happened today...it was temporary. It wouldn't last forever. "It's probably good practice. For Thanksgiving, I mean."

I don't remember when her hand sought out mine. At some

point, her pinkie was stroking mine. She turned a little so she was facing me. "Should we go upstairs now?"

———

UPSTAIRS, THE AWKWARDNESS SET IN. SHE'D FOLLOWED ME upstairs, her hand in mine. I kept thinking that maybe all of our interactions had been bound to lead to this moment. Even when I stopped to pick her up at the bus stop that rainy night, maybe even then I'd wanted to have her in my bed.

But once we'd crossed the threshold to my bedroom, every inch of me felt raw and exposed. I tried to go through the motions of my normal preparation for bed. I turned on the lamp on my bedside table. Keisha went to the front of the room and pulled closed the curtains.

She made the first move, hooking her thumbs in the waistband of the leggings she wore and drawing them down. She had her back to me and bent to step out of the leggings once they'd reached the floor. I watched, unable and unwilling to look away.

I had to force myself to turn away. Not because I didn't want to watch. I wanted to watch too much.

Maybe I wanted Keisha too much.

PART IV

NICK AND KEISHA - LIVES ENTWINED

12

KEISHA - WHAT A DIFFERENCE A DAY MAKES

S omething changed between us on Election Night. That night, we could have easily made love. We lay there in his bed, but we settled for holding one another. "I'm almost scared to kiss you," he'd admitted to me as we lay facing one another. His eyes were closed. I willed him to open them, to see me laying there topless, and to touch me. He'd tucked one hand under his pillow, the other lay still on my hip. His fingers pressed into my flesh, lightly at first.

"Look at me, Nick."

He did as I asked. I knew he worried about what would happen to our friendship. In a way, I worried too. I didn't want anything to disturb the balance...and yet, what I wanted most was to share my days and nights with him. I sometimes imagined what my life would have been like if I'd known him when I lived in New York, when my every waking hour focused on dance—on sewing elastic bands and thick ribbons to my pointe shoes, maintaining my flexibility and pushing myself to the limits to impress creative directors on the lookout for their next batch of principal dancers.

If I'd known him then...or if we'd met in London, would we have liked one another?

Would he still want me in his life?

Maybe all that mattered was the here and now. I didn't need to know if he'd been a jerk in his past if he'd learned from his mistakes. Maybe he didn't care that I'd been one of those dancers who didn't care about anyone else as long as I got the roles I wanted. Maybe we'd both fucked up and learned from every single mistake we'd ever made.

But now, when he looked at me with those eyes that sometimes revealed so much of the sadness and the joy and the fear inside him...all I wanted was to crush my lips against his and lose myself in his touch.

I took the lead. I initiated the kiss and took my time, savoring how Nick's breath came in rapid bursts, how his lips instinctively moved with mine. He pulled me closer and murmured, "What are we doing...?"

"Do you want to stop?" I traced the pad of my thumb along the curve of his lower lip. His smile came easily.

"No. Do you?" He captured my lips with his and teased me with the tip of his tongue.

"Definitely not..." I drew his hand upward from my hip. "I want more with you."

The touch of his hand warmed my skin, and when his thumb strummed my nipple, it tightened into a taut bud for him. I held his hand there until he dared to roll my nipple between his fingertips.

When he dared to stray from my lips to the tops of my breasts, I melted for him. I had the feeling I always would.

———

WE CAME SO CLOSE TO MAKING LOVE. WE FUMBLED, WE BUMPED noses, and burst into giggles; we inadvertently tickled one another and whispered "sorry" as if someone other than Rufus would overhear us. We fell asleep in one another's arms, woke up, and resumed kissing, and touching, and pleasing one another.

But...we didn't make love. Neither of us had prepared for this. We had no condoms, and though I had an IUD, we were both shy of taking a chance. We could wait, we reasoned. We knew we liked one another enough for this. We didn't have to rush. We had so much time...

But I wished we didn't have to wait. A part of me wondered if he was afraid of crossing the line because of the ghosts from his past.

But we had time and now, we knew we were both on the same page.

———

OLIVIA AND HANNES TEASED ME THE NEXT MORNING. I WAS dreamy through my warm-up. It was still early. I'd only had time to grab a quick cup of coffee before rushing to the studio.

"Someone either didn't get enough sleep last night or is in love," Hannes mused as the three of us stood at the barre going through the basic positions. "You have zero focus today."

"I had a late night," I said. "I had to work..."

Olivia shook her head and smiled at me. "Don't pay him any mind. You should have seen how he used to try to get my attention during our warm-ups and have Madame coming down on him for being unfocused. Didn't she call you imbecilic?"

"I'll never live that one down," Hannes laughed. He swept into a plié. "And for the record, we know you weren't working late. We had dinner last night at La Pêche."

"It's true, we did. The chocolate soufflé was so yummy..."

"Fine, fine..." I conceded. "I was hanging out with Nick last night. We were watching the election results."

"You're the only person we know who's smiling about that," Hannes quipped. "Makes me glad I still have my Swedish citizenship."

"I'm not smiling because of the results." I slapped at Hannes's arm. "I'm just really...happy."

"Love will do that to you," Olivia said as we moved into the next position.

I didn't say anything in reply. Instead, I focused on having perfect form as I moved into the next position. It was too soon to talk about love, but when I thought of Nick and when we were together, I felt like something wonderful and warm and bright filled me up.

Whatever this was that I was feeling carried me through a tense lunch shift at the restaurant, four hours of children's dance classes, and returning to La Pêche for the dinner shift when Malia called out sick.

It kept me smiling and feeling like I was floating on shimmering beams of sunlight, even when the news reports reminded us that the unthinkable had occurred. I let my mind drift back to our night together.

I needed something to hold onto in all of this craziness.

13

NICK - IT HAPPENED ONE NIGHT

W e slept together every night.

Whenever Keisha tried to retreat to the guesthouse, I stopped her with "Stay" and then kissed her into submission. We made out like teenagers, kissing until our lips were dry and swollen. We were sheepish. We were silly together. I didn't remember feeling like this before...at least not since I was still in high school.

I found myself wanting the house to be even homier for her. I put up curtains where there'd been bare windows. I drove to the nearest IKEA and bought rugs and cushions and bags of tea lights that I was sure I'd never use. But when Keisha saw them, she made sure we did.

I bought new pillows, cotton thermal blankets, and a new quilt for my bed. I moved my framed photo of April and me to the bedrooms I never used, the rooms I'd set up for Caitlin and Audrey, even though they would never be able to sleep there. I stopped short of emptying them and turning them into the guest rooms they should have been.

I couldn't do it yet. I still needed one place that was still a reminder of my life before.

But Keisha... I was pretty sure she was my future.

———

I DON'T KNOW WHAT I WAS THINKING, SUGGESTING THAT KEISHA pretend to be my girlfriend. It seemed like the perfect solution when I asked her, but now that we were on the road, little kernels of doubt were beginning to take shape. I gripped the steering wheel a bit too tightly. My knuckles shone white through my skin. Keisha could sense it; she was more talkative than usual, babbling about the new dance studio she'd found, and her running commentary was enough, temporarily, to prevent me from overthinking the lies I'd have to keep straight with my family. In the backseat, Rufus had been confined to a pet carrier, and he wasn't happy about it. The number of growls and howls he'd emitted, even with Keisha trying to bribe him with snacks and ear scratches, wasn't enough to satisfy the usually content canine.

We'd been on the road for around two hours, and already I was ill at ease. No one would believe we were a couple. Keisha was too gorgeous; why would she want to even be with someone who was so completely and utterly fucked? And my family would see this. They wouldn't buy that we were suddenly a couple—especially since I'd told Ellie when she was here that I wasn't sure when I'd ever be ready to date again. Wet snowflakes drifted down from the gray sky and splatted on the windshield. I had already started scanning I-95 for rest stop signs. I needed to get my head together. I needed a cigarette, and I hadn't smoked in months. Shit. Fuck. No, this was not good. Maybe we should turn around.

Then Keisha reached out and rested her left hand on my thigh. She let her index finger draw circles on my leg, leaving faint rings on my pants leg. "I know you're nervous," she said in a calm voice. "But you don't need to be. I've got your back. We'll be okay."

"They'll figure it out." I could almost picture my cousins scrutinizing us, pummeling us with blunt questions to break through our facade.

"Then let them," she retorted and smiled. "Let them think we're just friends; let them think we're having the most amazing sex together; let them think you're trying to figure out a way back to the old you. Let them think what they want."

"What if they're awful to you?"

"Do you think they will be?"

I shrugged. I honestly didn't know. I'd never brought home a Black woman before. With the way things were now, I didn't want to know which of my relatives had voted for Trump or thought that his brand of racism was acceptable. There'd been family dinners when my great-uncle Eamon railed against imagined slights he blamed on his Black neighbors. Some of my cousins blamed Obama for everything wrong with America —without thinking that they'd had tough times since the Bush-Cheney days. We'd always avoided getting into politics with them. Better to suffer in silence than to get harangued because we believed in climate change or thought that women had the right to decide if they were ready to have children. It had been the coward's way, but it kept family peace.

"Ellie will be nice to you. She's always nice. She likes everyone. Not sure about the others."

"We'll see. If they think you're happy, they're not going to want to make too big of a fuss." There was something in how relaxed she was that made me feel less...nervous. I wanted to believe her, but considering how weird the world we lived in felt these days, I still wasn't convinced.

"We'll leave, check into a hotel, and then drive home if everything..."

"We'll be fine. You, me, and Rufus. We'll be okay."

We'd already had a couple of people glare at us. Keisha ignored them, but I stared them down. I wasn't about to let them think they could get away with judging us when we weren't doing anything wrong. We were two friends who were going to spend Thanksgiving together. Sure, our skin colors were different, but that didn't change anything, not for me. So, who the fuck were they to try to make us feel uncomfortable about being together? Who the fuck were they to think that whatever we might be to one another was wrong?

Outside, the sky darkened with the promise of heavy rain or snow. It was so cold out that it would probably be freezing rain when it finally fell—unless the temperature dropped even more, and then it would snow. I hoped it would snow. Audrey and I loved Boston when it snowed. When she was a baby, I used to take her out in the stroller, bundled up in her snowsuit and thick fleece blanket, and we'd walk for hours. April hated it when I took Audrey out in the cold. She thought Audrey would catch a chest cold or the flu or something. But Audrey was like me, rarely ill and pretty resilient. Our evening walks continued until the night before she died. Maybe it was why I still liked walking. Rufus and I took our evening walks, and I sometimes imagined Audrey was with us, her small hand in mine, giggling and laughing as she told me about her day at school.

Then the snow arrived, at first, it was just light flurries, but then it came down in fat, wet clumps. I could barely see the road. I took the first exit I could. We weren't far from Baltimore. I think we were south of Baltimore-Washington International

Airport, and there was a rest stop with some fast-food restaurants and a hotel. We took a parking space as close to the hotel as possible. Just as I'd predicted, the wet snow froze as it hit the ground.

Rufus whimpered from his case. He was restless already and wanted out. Keisha peered up at the sky.

"Do you think this is going to turn into an ice storm?" she asked.

"Maybe," I said. "Depends, though. We could wait it out a while, see if it warms up a little. Then we could start driving again."

"Are we staying on I-95 the entire time?"

"Yeah, at least until just before we get to Boston."

"Good..."

"We could stop in Pennsylvania if you want."

"No...my parents know I am back, and they still haven't called me." She turned away. It was still a sore spot for her. She crossed her arms over her chest. I wished her hand was still on my thigh.

Behind us, Rufus scratched at the floor of his carrier and whimpered again. Keisha leaned back in the passenger seat and let out a sigh. Just then, I wished we weren't pretending we were together. If she were mine, I would take her in my arms and hold her against me, this delicate bird of a woman, and kiss her lips, the tip of her nose...I'd never let her go.

The realization jolted me. How long had I felt this way? I kept my emotions so tied to my life before. I couldn't just forget my wife, my daughters, even if there was this crackling of attraction between Keisha and me. Sometimes, just the nearness of her would set everything inside of me on fire. I had to walk away to quell my desire for her. I'd force myself to think of April, of her blonde hair that tumbled around her shoulders, how her startlingly blue eyes always caught me off-guard. I had to remember what I'd loved about my wife to keep myself from losing that love I had for her. I had to remind myself that I'd loved her to keep the guilt from eating me up inside.

How were we going to get through Thanksgiving at my sister's place?

Keisha pulled out her phone and began scrolling through the screens. "It says it's snowing pretty heavily from Philadelphia up to Boston."

"Great..."

"Should we see if we can get a room here, or do you want to keep driving?"

"We can try to get a room, see if they'll let us bring Rufus in."

"I can sneak him in. My bag is big enough to hold him," Keisha offered.

"No, we'll just ask. It's easier that way."

We took Rufus out of his carrier. Keisha bundled Rufus into her coat and then hurried into the hotel. I followed with our bags and made sure the car was locked. Inside, we managed to get the front desk staff to give us a pet-friendly room. The hotel was one of those cookie-cutter modern hotels—lots of beige walls, minimalist furniture in dark wood, and red and purple accents. I didn't care. I wasn't crazy about having to stay here, but at least we could ride out the storm, and it would give us some time to prepare for Boston.

———

OUR ROOM DIDN'T HAVE THE MOST INSPIRING VIEW—THE PARKING lot and the exit back to the highway. At least it was warm and clean and had all the modern amenities three snow-stranded travelers could need: two beds, a mini-bar stocked with decent quality wine and spirits, access to more cable channels than anyone needed, and WiFi. We'd be all right.

There were two queen-sized beds separated by a bedside table. Rufus claimed the bed closest to the window. I set our bags down by the bathroom door and looked around while Keisha opened the closet and looked for an extra quilt.

"There's one on the bed already," I told her as I unzipped my parka.

"I'm still cold, though." She was shivering, despite the heavy wool coat, hat, and scarf she'd thrown on before we left Richmond. "Maybe I'm coming down with something."

"We could always turn around."

"No, we promised Ellie," she said firmly. "We're only turning around if it gets worse than this."

I almost thought she wanted this more than Ellie. Sometimes, it was as if Keisha was on this personal mission to save me from myself. She'd already curbed my habit of drinking glass after glass of whiskey. I still wasn't sure how she'd done it. It had started with one of our marathon talks one night. She'd made a pot of tea for us, and we sat together on the couch, draining cup after cup as we shared our secret sorrows. I liked watching how she tested the tea with the tip of her tongue before daring to take a sip.

She had this thing about how she made the tea, how long she let the tea leaves steep and pouring a splash of milk in the cup first. "It doesn't make a difference," she confided as we let the hours slip away. "It will taste the same, but I like doing it this way."

There was something about that night, and the easiness of being with her that changed me. I wanted to be a different man with her.

———

BY DINNERTIME, THE SKY WAS SO THICK WITH SNOWFLAKES THAT
I-95 was closed between Richmond and Baltimore. According to
the Weather Channel, road conditions were worsening in
Delaware and eastern Pennsylvania as the whirlwind of snow
blanketed the east coast. We were truly snowed in. There was
no way we'd be able to get back on the road tonight. I fished
around in my coat pocket, found my phone, and called Ellie
with the news.

"If the snow lets up, we'll get on the road again in the morning," I said. "We might make a pit stop in Pennsylvania so
Keisha can see her parents."

"But you'll be here by Thanksgiving?" Ellie sounded hopeful. It made me smile. Maybe Keisha was right. Maybe Ellie just
wanted to see me happy. She wasn't trying to force me into
anything.

"We'll damned well try," I assured her. "It's Mother Nature
in charge, not us."

"You should have taken the train," Ellie complained. I could
hear her typing in the background. She was probably online,
checking Amtrak so she could advise me. "The trains are still
running...well, they're behind schedule but they are still
running."

"I promise, Elle, we're coming. We might wait until we're
heading back to Richmond to stop by her parents' place. It all
depends on the weather."

I went back over to the window and pulled back the curtain.
Snow blew across the parking lot in drifts. I could barely see my
car. Even if the snow stopped tonight, it would be a nightmare
getting out on the road again, but I didn't want to disappoint my
sister. And I needed to keep a promise to myself.

"Don't drive too fast," she warned. "You know what the roads are like up here."

"It's fine. I've got snow tires on the car."

"And you're really bringing your girlfriend?"

"I am..." I turned just as the bathroom door clicked open.

Keisha emerged from the room, wrapped in one of the complimentary guest robes, as I was finishing my call with Ellie. She'd braved the snow and wind to take Rufus out, and the two had returned while I was in the middle of the call. Rufus had probably been in his element in the snow. Border Terriers were such resilient dogs. Snow and cold weather were only minor predicaments for Rufus. Keisha, on the other hand, had looked frozen to the bone when they'd returned.

"I'll call you in the morning when we're on the road again." Once I ended the call, I plugged my phone into the charger.

"Better now?" I asked.

Keisha nodded and then crawled into the covers of her bed. "Rufus is insane. He wanted to stay out longer, but my feet were freezing."

"He's a little snow crazy." I grinned. I sat down on the edge of my bed. The floral scent of her shower gel lingered in the room. Rufus looked up from his position in the chair by the window. His little ears twitched. "Yeah, buddy, we're talking about you, you little snow monster."

I was sure Rufus gave me a side-eye before he let out one of his sighs and rested his furry chin on his paws. Knowing him, he'd fall asleep soon and treat us to his canine snores.

"I thought my shower would warm me up, but I'm still cold." She huddled deeper into the covers. "Rufus should come over here and at least warm up my feet, considering how long I was out with him."

Rufus showed no signs of leaving the armchair, though, especially since he had his favorite blanket and chew toy.

"I think you're out of luck with him. He's pretty much down for the count."

Her hand emerged from under the quilt. She patted the mattress. "Then you do it instead."

I didn't need her to ask a second time. I pushed myself off my bed and took the two steps necessary to climb into bed with her.

"Was that Ellie on the phone?"

I nodded as I fitted my body to hers under the thick layer of covers. "She still thinks we're not coming."

"It's understandable. You haven't been home in years."

"It's not home there anymore."

I swore to myself this was all platonic. There shouldn't have been anything sexy about being in bed with Keisha when I was still fully clothed and she was wrapped in so many layers. But from the moment I draped my arm around her, my pulse quickened. Keisha let me get comfortable. But even her stillness was turning me on. I knew if I slid my hand under the covers, past the bathrobe, I'd meet her bare skin, still warm from the shower.

Already I could smell the faint hints of vanilla and something floral on her skin, the damp heat rising from her hair and neck. Keisha had turned so her back was facing me. Even through the thick cotton of the bathrobe, I could feel the heat rising from her body. My body was already responding, but I thought if I lay perfectly still she wouldn't notice.

"Do you think Ellie will put us in the same room?" Keisha pressed against me. She had to feel how hard I was getting from being so close to her...

"Probably. It'll be a full house."

"We may as well get some more practice with being in the same bed then," she concluded. "Then no one will question us."

I curled my body around hers and felt her adjusting to accommodate me. Then she turned so she faced me and our lips brushed. A thousand little stars flared between us.

"Sorry..." she murmured. But then she licked her lips and I couldn't stop myself. I kissed her, pulled her closer to me, and let my tongue explore hers.

We pulled apart, just long enough to miss the feel of each other. "Is this okay?"

I nodded, letting my fingers slide along the curve of her neck. I pressed my lips there then, savoring the heat of her skin, the velvety warmth. I hadn't kissed anyone like this for so long. Kissing Keisha triggered something within me—the bleak realization that I'd been holding everyone at bay, protecting myself and thinking I would never need human touch, not after April. But now, someone else was touching me, running her fingers through my hair, pressing her body against mine, and triggering so many emotions in me I'd thought I'd lost with April's death.

I don't think either of us was sure when it shifted. When her robe was discarded or when the covers were pushed aside. I remembered stripping, anxious to be near her, opening her legs and tasting her, and loving how delicious it was to be so intimate with her, to anticipate her reactions and the bliss of her moans and sighs. She clutched at my hair, urged me to go deeper, to take all of her.

We explored each other's bodies, at first tentatively, and then with abandon. At one point, she was on top of me, riding me with such wantonness that I couldn't take my eyes off her. I gripped her hips; I was so drunk on the electric hot pleasure she was setting off in me. Damn, I was lost in her. I was lost and I didn't want to be found.

She came so hard she tightened around me and pulled me with her. We were both slick with sweat, our breaths hard and jagged and fast. She lay on top of me, pressing kisses to my neck while I held her close.

"That was..."

"...amazing...oh God, Nick. I want..."

"More...?"

She nodded. I could feel her smiling against my skin. I was still hard; I could keep going as long as she wanted me.

"I thought you said it was only ever me..."

I was still tangled in the bedsheets and Keisha's limbs. In the darkness, something shimmered and stirred the curtains. "April...?" I croaked. My throat felt rough and dry like sandpaper.

A sliver of light came through the curtains. I blinked and tried to push myself into a sitting position without disturbing Keisha. The shape by the window came into focus. "April...?"

I could barely make out her face, but the pale hair...and the whip of her voice still stuck in my mind... how long had it been since one of her ghostly visits? Weeks...months? I'd lost count. I'd almost stopped thinking of her.

"Are we over now?"

I didn't know what to say to her. *Babe, I'm sorry. I loved you for so long.*

"I thought it would always be me..."

I tried to form the words in my mouth. I wanted to tell her that I would always love her, but that I needed to be able to love again. I couldn't stay trapped in the bubble of drink and grief that had been my life.

Rufus growled and let out a hoarse woof. I shushed him. April still stood by the window, her form translucent in the sliver of light from the gap in the curtains. "I'll always love you, Nick. I know we weren't always kind to one another, but all I ever wanted was for you to be happy."

I watched her disappear, like an overexposed image melting into a film. Rufus growled again, but I distracted him by patting the bed. He jumped out of the chair and then ran to my side of the bed. Having him close, even now, took the edge off how unsettling April's visitations could be. I thought each time would be the last, but it never was. Maybe this time was different. Often she said nothing. She never said anything remotely like goodbye. But this time, it felt like maybe she'd unlocked the illusory chains that bound us to one another.

14

KEISHA - TAKE MY HAND

"What are you writing?" We'd stopped at a café not far from the town where I grew up. Since we weren't allowed to bring Rufus in, we chose a banquette by the window so we could see him. I'd ordered a hot chocolate with whipped cream and a slice of apple pie. Nick only wanted coffee.

"It's my homework for Dr. Sheridan." Nick didn't look up from the notebook he was scribbling in. He didn't often talk about the homework his therapist assigned to him. Once, though, he admitted that he didn't always do it, which exasperated his therapist. "I'm supposed to write down specific memories of April, of the girls, of our life before...and after."

"Does it help?" I stretched my hand across the tabletop and held his. It felt so good to touch him. After last night, I wasn't sure how things would be for us, but there was no awkwardness. Just us.

"Yeah, it does, I guess. I get it out of my head." He looked up now and smiled at me. I loved his crooked smile and his slightly off-center nose. I loved too how one of his front teeth was slightly chipped. It added to his scruffy ruggedness. It made him feel more real, more down to earth.

"What should you do with them once you've written everything down?"

He shrugged. "We haven't got that far yet, but I was thinking of burning them."

"But why?"

"I don't know. I guess it feels like a way of setting them free." Then he changed the subject. "You nervous about seeing your parents?"

"No." But that was a lie. I was. It wasn't my idea to come. Well, maybe it was. We were halfway to Pennsylvania when I had the bright idea to text my parents and wish them a Happy Thanksgiving.

I'd figured I could make the effort since I'd convinced Nick to do so with his family. What I hadn't expected was for my mother to call me and quiz me about where I was and how I was going to spend my holiday. I was still a little shell-shocked that my mother had answered my text.

Once I told her that I was going to Boston with a friend, she said very plainly, "Come by. Your father and I want to see you." And I knew it was more of a demand than an invitation.

Nick seemed more excited about it than I was. "I think it's great that you can do this. It's like we're both getting a chance to exorcise our ghosts."

"We'll see. It all depends on the reception we get."

"She must miss you. She asked you to come."

"I don't know, Nick. My parents...they're difficult."

"All parents are difficult," he said, shaking his head. "They know exactly which buttons to push."

"They do. And mine are expert at it."

"We're in this together." Nick took my fork and took a bit of my pie. "We keep saving each other."

"It's our schtick," I joked and reclaimed my fork. "Stop stealing my pie."

"Seriously, Keisha, if it's gets to be too much—even if the roads are shitty—we'll leave. Okay?"

I nodded yes. "Maybe we need a code word?"

"You just tell me you're ready, and then we go."

"Okay."

"So, what are their names?"

"Walter and Mathilda. But everyone calls my mother Maddie."

"Walter and Maddie. They sound like a sitcom couple."

"They're normal. They just..." I struggled to find the right words. It wasn't that my parents were horrible people. Far from it. They just never seemed very interested in me. And growing up with parents who often treated me like an afterthought had lefts its mark. "I don't think they like me very much."

"I'll bet it's nothing like that." Nick flashed one of his crooked smiles. It was one of my favorite things about him. And despite what he'd lost, he still tried to see the best in everyone. "I'll bet they'll be all kinds of happy to see you."

"We'll see."

He drained his coffee. "Are you ready?"

"As I'll ever be."

———

"I SUPPOSE YOU NEED A PLACE TO LAY YOUR HEAD TONIGHT." My father uttered the words without looking away from the television screen. Since we'd arrived, he hadn't so much as moved from his favorite armchair other than when my mother called us into the kitchen for dinner.

We'd arrived just after lunch and so far, it had been a strained, but not completely unpleasant, experience. None of us touched on the fact that we hadn't really spoken in years or that I'd been back in the States for a few months and this was pretty much our first real contact.

"Yeah, I guess we do." Not much had changed in all the years I'd been gone. The same framed school portraits still hung on the staircase wall. The same muffled silence blanketed everything. My parents barely spoke other than to ask one another questions or to share news of my estranged sister, Lolo.

Nick cleared his throat. "It's a little too late to get back out on the road, sir."

I knew he was right. It was already closing in on ten o'clock, and the weather still hadn't improved. When we'd arrived, the falling snow was more like flurries, but now it was coming down a little heavier. I tried to imagine us clambering back into the car with a restless Rufus and it didn't sound very promising, especially since the roads here had been pretty icy.

"Probably even slipperier now," my father agreed. He tapped his index finger on the remote and turned off the television. My mother was already upstairs. "Estelle, you may as well show him where the guest room is, give him some clean towels too."

I shushed Nick before he could question why my father called me Estelle. I would explain it to him later.

"Could we bring Rufus inside?" Nick rose to his feet. "He's always slept indoors...he's not used to sleeping away from me."

"Is he housetrained?"

"He is, sir."

"All right then." My father stood now too. "Estelle, go on and let the dog in from the backyard."

When I came back with a shivering Rufus in my arms, Nick and my dad were already on their way upstairs. Nick was carrying both of our bags; Dad was leading the way. I followed close behind, whispering to Rufus that soon he'd be warm under the covers.

Once upstairs, my father opened the first door to the right, my old bedroom, and turned on the ceiling light. "Everything's pretty much the same as you left it," he said. "New mattress, some new pillows. Otherwise, it's the same." I went inside and took in my past.

Framed posters of a young Peter Martins, Arthur Mitchell, and Carmen de Lavallade graced the walls, reminders of my dream of joining their ranks, even when I'd always known how difficult it would be. I felt as though time stood still. Here I was, twelve years old again, stretching and trying to improve my flexibility, saving my weekly allowance to purchase more toe shoes and leotards, even as my mother warned me that dance would only disappoint me.

The air in my childhood bedroom was still perfumed with traces of the lavender-scented fabric softener my mother used. I didn't know why this made me smile. Maybe it was because those moments in my room, when I used my dresser as a makeshift barre and practiced the five basic positions, had been moments of freedom for me. In my room, I dreamt myself away from Lancaster County and envisioned a more exciting life, playing principal roles in my favorite ballets on stages in New York or Paris or Vienna.

"I thought you would have taken all of this down by now," I said as I nuzzled Rufus. I wrapped him in the folds of my thick sweater.

"It's your room," was my father's reply. "It's here for you when you need it."

My mother eased past my dad with two extra quilts in her arms. The tight expression she'd worn had now softened. I could almost imagine she was pleased we'd come.

"It can still get a bit drafty in here," she explained as she set the quilts down on the twin bed closest to the window.

Then she gestured at Nick. "You can sleep on the extra bed in here. No point in putting you across the hall when I'm pretty sure you'll end up in here."

She said it so matter-of-factly, not at all like the last time I'd come home with a boyfriend. I pretended not to notice, but my father tensed. He didn't like the arrangement, but my mother had given the decree, and I knew he wouldn't contradict her in front of us.

"Thanks for letting us stay the night," Nick spoke up now as he stepped into the room. His voice sounded rough and tired as he set our bags on the floor near the closet. "With the weather conditions..."

"There's no way we would have sent you out into that weather again." My mother reached out and patted Nick's shoulder. "Get some rest now. Let's see what tomorrow brings us."

My parents wished us good night and then closed the door behind them as they left the room.

"So this is where you used to dream about being a ballerina," Nick teased. "Which bed was yours?"

I pointed at the one closest to the window. "I used to stare out the window at night and wish for so many things."

"You okay?"

Nodding, I kissed the top of Rufus's head. His scruffy fur

scratched my chin. "It feels weird to be here. I haven't been home...god, for years."

"Was it before you moved to London?"

"Yeah, I took the train down from New York." I went to my bed by the window and sat down. Rufus licked my cheek with his rough tongue then scrambled out of my arms and onto the bed. "I was so excited, I wanted to celebrate that I was starting a new phase in my life, that I'd gotten my big break and my career was going in the right direction."

Nick joined me on the bed. The mattress squeaked and groaned under our weight. We both laughed, but we didn't say a word. We still hadn't talked about what happened in the hotel. Maybe we didn't need to. Maybe it was enough knowing that, no matter what, we'd needed one another.

"We could turn around tomorrow," Nick said. "If the weather isn't on our side, we could just say fuck it and go back to Richmond."

It was tempting. After the chilly and somewhat stilted reception we'd initially received when we'd arrived here— despite my mother telling me she wanted to see me—returning to Richmond sounded so tempting. But...he'd promised his sister... and in the months we'd gotten to know one another, I'd learned that Nick hated breaking promises to her, and he'd already broken so many.

"I predict no snow in the morning and they'll have salted and sanded the roads."

"We'll see."

"We should get ready for bed."

"We should," Nick agreed. He grinned at me. "It's too bad we can't sleep in the same bed...or maybe that's a good thing."

"We couldn't...not here."

"You never snuck any boyfriends up here when you were a teenager?"

I shook my head no. "I wasn't allowed to date until I was sixteen or seventeen. And it wasn't like the guys in this town were lining up to ask me out."

"Why not?"

"We're in Amish country, Nick... and people out here in Mount Joy, they're...they didn't want their sons dating me, and their sons were more interested in giggly, blond cheerleaders— not ballet-obsessed Black girls."

"They were stupid then."

The mattress sagged a little under our weight. I licked my lips and wondered if he'd kiss me. Or would he suddenly decide he needed to brush his teeth and call it a night?

"Why'd your dad call you Estelle?"

Of course, he remembered. "It's the name they gave me when I was born." I reached out to tickle Rufus's paw, but Nick caught my hand in his. "I legally changed my name to Keisha when I moved to New York."

"But why?"

"It sounds like an old woman's name. I hated being called Estelle," I nearly groaned. I hated that name."

"It doesn't really suit you." He leaned in and kissed me. "No, you don't kiss like an Estelle."

"We can't..."

"I know...I have the feeling your parents have supersonic hearing."

"They do. They hear everything."

"And you're too loud anyway."

"It's not my fault." I held back the smile threatening to curve my lips. I loved this...the way he teased me when I least expected it. I leaned in, greedy for another chance to kiss him.

This time, I took the lead and kissed him until his soft lips opened under mine. With each touch, a flare of longing and recognition that he was the man I wanted, even when I knew there was so much potential for all of this to go horribly wrong.

We were like moths drawn to the light, unable to resist the alluring brightness.

We could have gone kissing one another; we were so caught up in the moment. But Rufus perked up, jumping to his feet and growling just as someone knocked on the door. I pulled away reluctantly and went to the door while Nick lowered his head and grinned.

When I opened the door, my mother handed me a set of washcloths and bath towels. "I nearly forgot about these," she said. Then she touched my cheek. "I know I didn't say this earlier, but I'm glad you decided to come."

"Me too," I admitted.

"Your boyfriend seems nice."

"He is."

She seemed ready to say more, but instead, she hugged me and pressed a kiss to my cheek. "Get some rest. We'll talk more in the morning."

I nodded okay and kissed my mother again before I closed the door. Even if it still felt surreal to be here, I needed to be here, if only to prove to myself that I could come home again.

DESPITE ANY URGES WE MIGHT HAVE HAD, WE SLEPT IN SEPARATE beds. Rufus chose to curl up at the foot of my bed, which pleased me, especially since it meant he kept my feet warm. But I woke suddenly from a dream that Nick had gotten cold feet and left me and Rufus behind as he retreated to Richmond. My heart was beating wildly; I could barely catch my breath. I remembered calling out to him as his car disappeared in a hazy cloud of snow and pale sunlight.

"I'm here..." His voice was still heavy with sleep. He reached across the divide between our beds. I stretched out my hand and found his in the darkness. His reassuring warmth surrounded me. "I'm here, Keisha..."

"I dreamt you left me," I whispered as I pulled my quilt tighter around me. "You didn't even say goodbye."

"That'll never happen," he said hoarsely. "I won't ever leave you. I promise."

———

THE FIRST THING I NOTICED WHEN I WOKE WAS HOW QUIET THE house was. My cold feet let me know that Rufus had abandoned the bed. Nick's bed was empty. His pajamas lay in a heap on top of his weekender bag. He'd probably taken Rufus out for his morning walk, but waking up to an empty room reminded me too much of my dream.

I tried to shake the pall of it as I showered and changed into a pair of jeans, some thick, wool rag socks, and a chunky knit sweater I'd liberated from Nick's closet before we left Richmond. Downstairs, my father was in the kitchen filling the coffee maker. There was no sign of my mother or of Nick and Rufus.

"Good morning, sleeping beauty." My dad set two empty mugs on the table. "Sit down. You look like you're still stuck in dreamland."

Maybe I was. Being back still felt unreal. I kept going over in my mind my last visit when neither of my parents had been particularly happy to see me. We'd argued most of that visit about my impending move to London. In hindsight, I knew their anger was motivated by fear—I was supposed to be the reasonable daughter, the reliable one, and I'd scoffed at the stability they'd worked so hard to give me.

"Where is everyone?"

Dad pulled out a chair and joined me at the table. "Your boyfriend got up early and took his dog out, then he came back and shoveled the sidewalk. Now, your mom's gone for a walk with them."

From outside, we could hear the scrape and drone of the snowplows clearing the streets.

"Where's Lolo?" Lolo was my older sister. Her real name was Eloise, but no one ever called her that. For as long as I remembered, she'd always gone by Lolo. While I'd loved dance, Lolo adored numbers. When we were younger, she never followed our parents' rules. She was the one who snuck out of the house at night to take the train to Philadelphia to go to concerts or disappeared for days at a time only to return and announce that she'd gone to New York on a whim. Her antics meant my parents were much stricter with me. But she was the one who'd eventually toed the line and become an accountant.

"She's in Pittsburgh for the holidays."

"Does she have to work?"

"No, your sister's engaged." My dad tapped his palm on the tabletop. "She's getting married in June. I guess she didn't tell you."

"We don't really talk," I reminded him. We never had, not really. We'd grown up together, but we'd never had that closeness so many of my friends had with their sisters. We were more like strangers who shared DNA and were raised by the same people.

"No, I didn't think you did. You don't talk to us much either."

"Come on, Dad. You guys made it pretty clear you didn't approve of my dancing." It still rankled me. I'd been the one who was the good daughter, the one who always brought home good grades and never gave them cause to worry at school, but I was the rebel because I'd chosen dance and the arts over a practical life.

"Estelle—"

"My name is Keisha, Dad. I wish you would just call me that instead of Estelle. That's never been my name."

"It's the name your mother and I gave you."

"I never felt like an Estelle...I don't get it—why is it okay that Eloise can call herself Lolo, but I can't have a name that feels more like me?"

"Estelle..."

"Keisha. My name is Keisha."

"We don't want to fight with you all the time."

"Then why does it always feel like you do? You don't approve of anything I do. You didn't support me..."

"We paid for all of those damned dance classes you wanted to take."

"No, you didn't, Dad." I pushed away from the table and stalked to the other side of the kitchen. I needed coffee if we were going to get into it. I didn't even want to have this discussion, but it was bound to happen, wasn't it?

"I gave you an allowance—"

"You paid for my lessons until I was eleven. Then you told me that you weren't wasting your hard-earned money on something that wasn't going to pay the bills," I reminded him as I filled my mug with coffee. "After that, I went around the entire neighborhood asking everyone for odd jobs just so I could earn enough to pay for the lessons myself."

"Then you learned a good lesson."

"Don't talk to me about lessons, Dad. You paid for everything Lolo ever wanted. But you and Mom always made me feel like what I wanted was ridiculous or unnecessary."

"You know that's not true."

"You didn't even show up when I graduated from Julliard," I scoffed. "My God, I went to the best school for the arts in the goddamn country, and you wouldn't even come to see me perform or get my diploma."

"Keisha, now, that's not fair. You know your sister had that car accident."

"It was a fender-bender, Dad. She wasn't even seriously injured. She didn't even need to stay at the hospital, but neither of you could leave her side. I thought one of you would at least show up." I tried not to raise my voice, but I could hear my frustration fuelling it, straining for release. "And when I got injured and called for advice, you didn't even listen. You and Mom gave me hell about following my dream and said I knew what I was getting into when I moved overseas. I was laid up in a hospital in London with screws holding my knee together, and neither of you seemed to care."

Now that the floodgates had burst open, I let all the frustration and anger rush forth. Every inch of me vibrated with pent-up hurt at how I'd always been made to feel that I was not valued by my family. My father tried to interrupt, but I didn't let him get a word in. I needed him to hear this. My whole life I'd felt like I could never be me because my parents gave me no space in their life. And even now as an adult, I wanted them to give me a sliver of space that was mine, but...at least my father... only understood the old roles.

"You got to know how much your children need you. You ever have your own kids, you'll see. There's always one who needs you more than the others. The one who seems like she is strong but is fragile as a piece of china inside. And that child wasn't you, Keisha. It was Lolo."

"I needed you, too, Dad."

"Your sister couldn't get her head together. Your sister can't make a decision without checking it three-four times with us." Dad tapped his finger on the tabletop. "But you...you make a decision, and you just do it. You never waited for us to tell you what to do. You already knew what you wanted. So, we set you free. We wanted you to be independent even if it scared the hell out of us."

I sat in stunned silence. I didn't know what to say. They'd thought the space they'd given me was independence while I'd felt abandoned and unloved. How did I even respond to that?

I barely heard Nick and my mother's return. I was still standing at the counter, clutching my now-empty coffee mug and staring at the chair and the half-drunk mug of coffee my father had abandoned when he'd decided he'd had enough of listening to me. He was in the living room now, blocking me out with the snapping of the pages of the newspaper.

My mother and I ended up working together, preparing breakfast without speaking of anything important. A few times, she touched my hair or placed a hand on my shoulder in a way so full of maternal love that it made me want to cry. She had never really been like this when I was younger. Or maybe she had, but I saw it all through the fog of parental criticism—the tugging at my skirts when they were deemed too short, the pinching of my arm and proclaiming me too skinny when they'd known dancing used up all the energy I put into my body.

Once breakfast was ready, the four of us sat together at the kitchen table. This time, Rufus wasn't relegated to the pantry. I tried to extend an olive branch to my dad by asking about how the Eagles were doing. It broke the icy silence enough for him to admit that he was pleased as punch that the team seemed to have overcome last year's slump. He and Nick ended up talking football, while my mother asked about what I was doing now that I was in Richmond with Nick.

"I'm dancing again," I told her. "Not professionally but teaching dance to children."

"You're going to be in the Nutcracker," Nick reminded me. "That's pretty big."

"It's a small performance," I said. "It's just one night. We're raising money for charity."

"But that's wonderful." My mother looked genuinely pleased. "When will it take place?"

"The ninth of December." Nick reached for the bowl of hash brown potatoes and took another spoonful. "You should come down. I can fix some tickets for you. And we have plenty of room."

I pressed my lips together to stop myself from saying no. I was sure they'd brush aside his offer, but instead, my father said, "We'd like that. We've never had a chance to see Est... Keisha dance on stage."

Under the table, Rufus licked my hand. He leaned against my leg and reminded me that I had a small family now, even if it wasn't traditional. Nick, Rufus, and I were a little family. And now, my own family...well, hopefully, this peace would last.

Maybe things would be smoother from here on.

———

"What happened while I was gone?"

"Nothing." I winced at how petulant I sounded. I tried to focus on the scenery—we'd just merged onto the Pennsylvania turnpike. Snow-blanketed hills dotted with black trees. From the backseat, Rufus let out an exasperated harrumph. He didn't know how lucky he was. He didn't have to deal with the labyrinth of family problems. At least by the time we left, the weird mood had broken, and my parents both seemed genuinely happy we'd come by.

"Keisha, c'mon, obviously something happened. You and your dad—I felt like I stumbled into a cold war."

"I don't want to talk about it. Not yet, anyway."

"Fair enough."

"At least your invitation made things better," I conceded.

"When we were out walking Rufus, your mom kept talking about how she'd watched videos of your performances on Youtube."

"She never told me that." I tried to hide my surprise. "She never told me anything good about my dancing."

"Hey..." We'd stopped now at a traffic light. "Look at me, Keesh."

When I did, he leaned in and kissed me softly enough to silence any more words. His fingers curled in my hair as he pressed another, longer kiss to my lips.

The light changed; someone behind us honked their horn and interrupted the moment. But even as I settled back into the passenger seat, the feel of his lips on mine remained, and I couldn't stop smiling.

We'd been driving for an hour now without speaking. I checked the GPS instead. If the road conditions were okay, we'd make it to Worcester in around six hours. So far, the roads were plowed. The sunshine we'd seen earlier had disappeared behind thick clouds again. I'd already checked the weather report before we left. Snow was still in the forecast. This was just a brief pause the weather forecaster warned from the radio,

"Be prepared for another six to eight inches, possibly up to a foot of snow in some areas."

Nick didn't press for more information, though he shot furtive glances my way. I could almost hear him working through his thoughts, wondering how to broach the subject without upsetting me. A part of me wished we'd stayed in Richmond. I was the one who'd convinced him this road trip was a good idea. And even if the visit with my parents had not been the hell I'd expected, I still wished I'd just suggested Thanksgiving at home, just the three of us.

I turned so I could see him. He'd forgotten to shave, and his beard was getting a little too long. I reached across the distance between us and stroked his cheek. He relaxed under my touch. Somehow, all felt right with us again.

15

NICK - NEARLY THERE

We were only an hour from Worcester, but I had to pull over. I took the first rest stop—it was nothing more than a strip mall with a Starbucks and some fast-food restaurants—and parked at the far end of its parking lot. Keisha had fallen asleep somewhere near Connecticut. I'd grabbed the blanket from the backseat and draped it over her. Rufus, well, he nearly always dozed off in the car.

While they slept, I paced and chain-smoked. It was fucking frigid. I'd forgotten how cold it could get here. We were close enough to the ocean that I could practically smell its wet, salty tang.

My phone buzzed in my coat pocket, vibrating against my chest. I shivered against a gust of icy, wet air. I didn't need to check my phone to know it was Ellie calling. She'd been asking for progress reports since we left Pennsylvania. I'd sent a couple —one just after leaving Keisha's parents' house and another when we were on I-95 North heading toward the George Washington Bridge.

This was the nearest I'd been to Boston since I'd gone into my self-imposed exile. The sun was already setting, and the clouds were thickening. If I were alone, I would have turned the car around and driven south, back to Richmond, away from the memories waiting for me in Massachusetts. I was shaking. The ghosts of my previous life shimmered in the distance. I could just see Audrey kneeling in the snow, meticulously forming the foundation of a snowman, her favorite pink and yellow scarf wound around her neck. And Caitlin...skipping in the snow, unbothered by the flakes fluttering down from the sky. She shaded her eyes from the glare of headlights from an SUV pulling into the parking lot, and then she and her sister dissipated, vanishing into the puff of snow dust that flew up from the car tires.

I shook my head...no. I couldn't go there. Not to the place where the ghosts awaited. I couldn't hold them at bay with whiskey. I couldn't let myself get sucked into the darkness.

"Nick?" Keisha was standing by the car. She stamped her feet on the frozen ground and tucked her gloved hands in her pockets. "Is everything okay?"

"Yeah, I'm fine." Damn, she was a sight for sore eyes. Sleepiness still clouded her eyes, and her slow smile at my approach made me want to take her in my arms and hold her for as long as she'd let me. "I was getting cold feet. That's all."

"Of course, you are. It's freezing out here." She glossed over my fear, took hold of my hands, and pulled me close.

"I just needed a break." I slung an arm over her shoulder and folded her into me. Her hair tickled my chin. She wrapped her arms around my waist. Her breath warmed my skin. I didn't want to let go of her.

"You don't have to be scared, Nick," she said now. "We're a team, you and me. And Rufus. We'll get through this together."

"Okay..."

"How far are we from Ellie's place?"

I shrugged, though I knew without needing to even think about it. "An hour, I guess."

"Have you called her? We should probably let her know where we are."

I shook my head no. "I'll do it once we're back in the car."

I let my arm tighten around Keisha. She turned her face up to mine and smiled. My beautiful ballerina. How had I gone so long without ever having her in my life? I couldn't resist her. The only thing I wanted was to kiss her and taste the sweetness of her lips. So, I let go of her long enough to take her face in my hands, to let my fingertips graze her cheeks as my lips claimed hers. She moaned against my mouth. Her hot breath felt so sweet.

Somewhere behind us, a car horn honked, and the wind carried with it the oceanic whirr of passing cars. A car door slammed, and footfalls crunched on the icy snow.

"If you're gonna fuck her, get a room."

I ignored the three men laughing as they walked past us. They didn't know how good it was to hold her. We hadn't held one another like this since the night at the hotel. Last night, as we lay in separate beds at her parents' house, I'd wanted so badly to kiss her, to lie beside her at night and listen to the sweet, steady rhythm of her breathing as she drifted to sleep, to feel her hand squeeze mine as we held one another. Twice I'd nearly climbed into bed with her, but every movement produced a high-pitched squeak and a thunderous groan. Instead, I'd lain in that narrow twin bed, feverish with this longing to be close to her, too wired to fall into a deep sleep, too exhausted to keep my eyes open.

When she'd cried out my name, I'd woken instantly and

held out my hand to her. The moment her fingers found mine, I relaxed. I could have held her hand all night, but then she drifted off again, and her hand slipped from my grip.

I'd waited a while and then whispered, "I think I love you, Keisha. It's probably too soon to even say it, but I think it's true."

My confession evaporated into the night. I hoped she heard it. But even if she didn't... I would tell her again. I would tell her as many times as I could until she loved me too.

––––––––––

"I NEED SOME TIME ALONE WITH YOU BEFORE WE GO TO ELLIE'S." We were back in the car now, heading closer to my old life. Rufus was whining from the pet carrier. I hated putting him in it, but we could only safely travel this way with my sometimes-rambunctious dog. We'd left the interstate behind and closed in on Marlborough, the town where Ellie now lived.

If I just followed the road we were on, we'd be there in thirty minutes. But...I pulled to the side of the road. We were on a road that cut through an icy swatch of woods. Black branches curved overhead, forming an arch that blocked out the street lamps' glow. My chest tightened; it almost hurt to breathe. I was so close to my goal. All the energy drained out of me. I slumped forward, still gripping the steering wheel, and rested my forehead on my hands.

"Nick...Nick, we can do this together. It's us against the world, right?" Keisha scooted closer to me. Her warmth surrounded me as she slid her arms around me. "You can do this. You can see your family again and break bread with them...and it'll be okay because you have Rufus and me there."

Her touch calmed me. I didn't tell her about the ghosts following us. She knew a little already. I didn't want my life to be haunted forever. That was part of our coming here, wasn't it? To put the ghosts to rest? They'd been with me so many years. Maybe I didn't know how to live without them.

She coaxed me to turn my face to hers. Our noses bumped as we came together. At first, I thought she would only whisper encouragement to me, but she kissed me slowly, softly; her lips were like the faintest feathers on mine. I breathed in her scent, let my desperation for her take over as I pulled her so close; she gasped.

"Sorry..." I murmured against her lips. I let go of the wheel and slid my hands inside her coat. I wanted to be nearer to her. I wanted to be so close we could get lost in one another again. I wished we could go back in time, to when it was just us snowed in, in the hotel room, loving one another.

"Don't be. Just know I'm here for you. And we'll get through this together."

16

KEISHA - DESTINATION

"Oh my God, you really are here!"

The woman who greeted us had to be Nick's sister. As she latched onto him, tears streamed down her face, leaving a sooty trail of mascara on her cheeks. I stepped aside, Rufus squirming in my arms. Now that we were here, I didn't know what to do. I set him down and watched him prance around, waiting for Ellie to greet him too. She ruffled his fur and spoiled him with a doggy treat she'd hidden in her sweater pocket.

I unzipped my coat and unwound my scarf. Ellie was babbling at a shell-shocked Nick. I wanted to take his hand in mine, remind him he would be okay. But now, reunited with his sister, Nick still wore the look of someone a little lost, but he hugged his sister just as hard as she was hugging him.

"Ellie...Ellie... you should—I want you to meet Keisha," he said as he finally stepped out of his sister's embrace. The color was returning to his cheeks now. He came to me, took my hand, and pulled me forward.

I lifted my other hand in greeting. "It's nice to meet you finally."

Tears were still rolling down Ellie's cheeks. She wiped at them with the back of her left hand, the diamond setting of her engagement ring catching the light with the gesture.

"Nick kept talking about you, but I honestly thought he'd made you up so that I would leave him alone." Ellie took my hand now and squeezed it. "Thank you so much for convincing him to come."

"I didn't want him to break his promise to you," I said. Rufus was still prancing around us, his tail wagging wildly as he tried to see who would pet him or give him a treat.

"You guys must be freakin' exhausted." Ellie was on a roll now. "Hang your coats up here... are you hungry?"

"I could eat," Nick said as he shrugged out of his parka. I did the same and then slipped my feet out of my boots. It felt good to finally take them off after hours in the car.

I thought there would be more people here, but the house was remarkably quiet save for the television on in the living room.

"I told everyone to wait until tomorrow to come," Ellie explained as she led us through to the kitchen. "I thought maybe we needed a little breathing space."

Nick nodded. "We do. I don't know if I could have dealt with everyone at once."

"That's what I thought." Ellie gestured for us to sit at her kitchen island. I hadn't expected such a large kitchen. The room seemed to run the width of the house and looked newly renovated. The modern, deep grey cabinetry contrasted with the house's colonial redbrick exterior. Octagonal tiles in a pale shade of green served as the backsplash while the walls were a creamy beige. I climbed onto one of the barstools at the island. Nick was looking around, a little stunned.

"You didn't tell me your house was so nice," he joked, but he was still glancing around as if he expected someone else to walk in.

"I'm a working woman," Ellie said as she started the electric kettle. "I'm making you some tea to warm you up. I've got some chicken pot pie and mashed potatoes here and some salad."

"That sounds delicious."

My stomach rumbled at the thought of a home-cooked meal. We hadn't really eaten anything since we'd left my parents' house. I'd forgotten the sandwiches my mother made for us on her kitchen table. Nick only bought coffee when we'd stopped for a quick bathroom break at a rest stop in New Jersey, but I think then both of us had been too anxious to eat anything.

Ellie took care of everything. When I offered to help, she shushed me away and told me to relax, but it was hard to sit still while she rushed around, warming up food, grabbing plates and flatware, and pouring tea and then a glass of wine for herself. Through it all, Nick didn't say much. He looked as if he was bracing himself for an interrogation.

"Is it okay if I use..." I gestured at the doorway. Ellie gushed out "of course" and showed me where the guest bathroom was, tucked under the stairs in the space I'd merely assumed was an extra coat closet or catchall.

I needed a few moments to myself to process everything. Now, we were here...at least we were in the same state as the horrible memories Nick was trying to leave behind. I turned on the faucet and rinsed off my hands under the flow of warm water. I knew Ellie had questions, and she wouldn't ask them with me there.

"Does she know about what happened to April and the kids?"

"She knows."

"Are you going to visit them? April's parents?"

"They know I'm here?"

"Her mom called me a couple of days ago."

"What did you tell her?"

"I told her that you were trying to move on. It is what you're doing, right? With her?"

"She has a name."

"I know she does. I'm okay with you being with her, you know. I like her already."

"I like Keisha too."

"You must. The brother I know doesn't like holding hands with anyone."

"She makes me happy."

I shouldn't have been eavesdropping, but to hear Nick say that I made him happy…it filled me with this intense joy. I loved being with him. Sometimes, I'd been more afraid that he'd merely accepted that I was around; other times, I understood that we were connected.

We were only supposed to be pretending we were a couple, but it was too late for that, wasn't it? Especially when I knew I'd fall apart if we ever walked away from one another.

———

LATER, WHEN IT WAS JUST THE TWO OF US IN THE BACK BEDROOM Ellie had sworn was always intended to be Nick's room if he ever visited, Nick and I lay in bed together under the reassuring weight of the comforter and thick blankets. Despite the hot air pumping out of the central air vents, a chilly draft permeated the room. I was glad for the flannel nightshirt I'd packed, but Nick unbuttoned it as soon as we were under the covers.

"I want to feel your skin," he grumbled as his fingers worked on the last button. "It's the only way I know this is real."

"It's real," I assured him, raking my fingers through his hair. His left hand cupped my right breast, his thumb tracing circles around my exposed nipple. I bit my lip, holding in the moan elicited by his touch. "We should stop..."

"Why?"

"Your sister..." I breathed out.

"She's asleep...and I need you."

"I need you too..."

"Then we'll be quiet."

"We can try..."

I gave in. It wasn't as though I didn't want this. I almost needed to be close to him to feel like all of this was real. Ever since we'd arrived, my nerves felt awry. I kept telling myself it was because we were in unknown territory. The storm had allowed us to cross all the boundaries we'd previously maintained. Now we were free-falling, stumbling our way in this emotional minefield, paying no heed to what would happen next. But did it really matter? We could never know what the future had in store for us, but one thing I knew was that when he was inside of me, I felt so full of love and longing. Each slow stroke shattered me and left me whispering his name and begging for more.

I tried not to let my moans escalate, but when he lifted his hips just so...and he rubbed against my clit until it was so sensitive I was trembling, my fingers scratching at the sheets...my breath coming hot and heavy and ragged. He closed his eyes as he thrust into me and picked up the pace. The bed frame squeaked loud enough that Rufus growled and barked before going quiet again.

We were both panting...Nick braced his forearms now on either side of me and nipped at my lower lip then slid his tongue in between my parted lips and teased me with long, slow kisses that set fire to my blood and intensified my desire for him.

I loved the weight of him on top of me, how each time his chest grazed mine, my body seemed to flare. I strained to get closer to him, even when it felt that our skins were fused.

Nick's mouth came crashing down to mine again, claiming my lips with slow, deep kisses that I never wanted to end; his rough beard scratched my skin. I ran my hands down his toned sides until I could take hold of his hips and press him deeper still inside of me. My thighs ached, but I didn't care. I wanted more...even when I knew his sister could probably hear us from her bedroom down the hall, even when I was struggling to hold in every sigh, whisper, and moan.

I would always want more of him.

17

NICK - TWO HEARTS

How did I ever live my life without her? I thought as I lay in bed beside her, sated, truly happy for what was probably the first time in...years? How had I managed to get through the years of darkness and living with ghosts?

The house was still quiet. It was early yet—the sun hadn't risen, and from the sound of faint scratching at the windows, the snow had returned. I turned over carefully. I didn't want to wake Keisha. She was still asleep, with one arm curled around her while the other was tucked under her pillow. I adjusted the layers of blankets around her.

We weren't alone in bed now. At some point in the night, Rufus had abandoned the dog bed Ellie had bought just for him and hopped up on our bed. He was stretched out at the foot of the bed. One of his legs twitched.

Maybe he was dreaming about chasing rabbits.

I managed to get out of bed without disturbing either of them and went to the window. Snow blanketed the backyard, cloaking the hedges and forming white dunes. More had come during the night.

It reminded me of one Christmas Eve we'd spent with April's grandparents. They didn't live in Boston. They had a farmhouse in Pepperell, and it was the one place where I felt like I belonged as far as her family was concerned. It was a proper working farm, where her grandfather grew organic vegetables and raised free-range hens and turkeys. Audrey and Caitlin loved going there—they were still young enough to see the animals as pets and not food, or maybe they understood and never said a word to us about it.

But that Christmas Eve, April and I had argued all the way there. I'd been the one pushing to spend Christmas there—she'd wanted to stay in Boston with her parents. But I wanted the girls to have a country Christmas with snow and long walks and warming up afterward by the open fire. By the time we arrived, none of us was feeling very Christmasy. As we drove up the long driveway, however, and saw how thick and heavy the snow was that covered the fields and the rooftops of the house and the barns, we forgot about the japes and the petty words we'd slung at one another and let the snowy view charm us.

Before we could even go inside, Audrey and Caitlin took advantage of the moment to make snow angels. Our argument melted away as we watched our daughters playing in the snow. And their happiness stayed with us, carrying us through the holiday even when our marriage was falling apart before my eyes. Just remembering the joy and the overpowering sense of love I had for my daughters was what had brought me home every night.

———

Ellie was already awake and sitting in the living room watching the news with the volume turned down low. She turned her head and acknowledged me with a nod. "I think the snow's finally going to stop," she said as I slumped onto the sofa with her. "It might just be us for dinner, though. No one wants to chance the roads, even if they want to see you."

"This won't be the last time."

"You promise?"

I nodded. "I thought I'd feel them everywhere, but now it seems so far away."

"You should call her parents."

"April's?" I hadn't seen them since just before I moved back to Richmond. Once or twice a year, Emily sent me a letter, usually close to the girls' birthdays. I'd stopped reading them. Whenever they arrived, I stuck them in a drawer. I was tired of being blamed for their deaths.

"I think they'd like to hear you're okay."

"I need to move on with my life."

"That's what they want for you, Nick. We all want it." Ellie took my hand in hers and held it tightly. "I want you to be happy again. And I'm so glad you found someone who makes you smile again. Even if it means I hear you getting it on in my guest bedroom."

Above us, the floorboards creaked. Either Ben, Ellie's boyfriend, was awake or it was Keisha.

"Sorry about that."

"I don't care, Nick. It's fine. Honestly, it is. I am so glad you're here." Her eyes were getting shiny again. I hoped she wasn't going to cry. We didn't need any more tears. "I'm so glad you're back in the land of the living again."

It didn't take long that the sound of four paws scrambling down the steps alerted us to Rufus being ready for a walk and food. He was dragging his leash behind him and zigzagging around the living room, hedging his bets on which of us would take him out. Keisha came down a few minutes later, already dressed and calling for Rufus to meet her at the front door.

She paused at the bottom of the stairs when she finally noticed that Ellie and I were in the living room.

"I'm going to take that barrel of monkeys for a walk," she said as she managed to get Rufus to sit still long enough for her to attach his leash to his collar. "Is there a dog run nearby, Ellie?"

"No, unfortunately not. If there weren't so much snow, you'd be able to follow the path in the woods behind the house."

"I'll just go around the block with him then."

"I could come with you," I offered as I stood. I liked this feeling, of wanting to be with someone again, of wanting to be with Keisha all the time.

"I wouldn't say no to that," Keisha said with a smile. "But you should spend some time with your sister."

"He's sick of me already," Ellie pretended to pout. "You two go. I'll start breakfast."

"I'm not...I just need a walk and some fresh air is all."

"Go," Ellie insisted. "I know you won't disappear on me."

Once we bundled into our coats and winter gear, Keisha, Rufus, and I set off for our walk. Though Ben and I'd shoveled the sidewalk last night, more snow had fallen and blanketed the street. Rufus hopped in and out of the snow dunes lining the curb. It was a good thing he was a border terrier. His double layer of fur made him nearly impervious to the elements. He liked diving in the snow. Sometimes, only his hind legs stuck out from whatever snow hill he found to conquer. He'd emerge with a twig or frosty mustache and an excited bark.

Thick, heavy snow covered every surface. There was hardly

any traffic on the roads. The snowplows were only just beginning to make headway.

I'd remembered this from my childhood and then the years
I'd spent here in Massachusetts with April and the girls. Snowy
winters. Days on end when falling snow seemed never-ending.
Caitlyn and Audrey loved it. They could spend hours playing in
the snow, clad in their waterproof snowsuits, their cheeks rosy
from the cold. They'd only come indoors when hunger hit
them or if we called them inside to warm up.

"How does it feel now?" Keisha ventured carefully on the
patches of clear sidewalk. She tested for iciness before continuing forward. "You seem...relaxed."

"It's hard to explain..." I started, but the words, how I felt,
what all of this meant, seemed inadequate. "I thought the
ghosts would follow me, hang over me."

"Do you still see them?"

"Sometimes. But it's different now. When I see April, the
anger is gone. It's like she's accepted that I can move on."

"Did you see her a lot?"

"It's usually Caitlyn and Audrey that come to me. Audrey
especially." So many memories swirled inside of me. All of the
times I caught glimpses of my children when it was impossible.
"Audrey and I had this special bond. She was the one who
always held my hand. She always came to me when she
couldn't sleep or had nightmares. It used to drive April crazy. I
think she wanted to be everything for Cait and Auds, but my
baby girl always came to me."

Above us, snow-laden branches creaked in the wind. Rufus
barked for us to get moving again, so we let him lead us further
along the road. As we walked, our hands bumped and brushed
one another. I flexed my fingers out and took hold of hers. I
didn't miss the smile Keisha tried to hide.

"Do you think your parents will come to Richmond?" I hoped they would. Keisha needed more time with them. They still had so much baggage that they needed to work through. At least I had Dr. Sheridan and her infernal homework to help me sort things out in my mind. As much as I hated it, it did help.

"I don't know." Keisha licked her lips and then pressed them together. It was one of her nervous tics. Maybe she was afraid to believe in the truce they'd reached. "I was thinking...I should send them tickets once we're home again. Give them an incentive."

"I think they'll love seeing you on stage."

"It's no big deal, though. It's just something we're doing for the kids."

"For me, it is. I get to see you on stage—and not just in blurry YouTube videos. I'll bet it will be the same for them."

"Maybe..." but she was smiling again.

We continued onwards, with Rufus showing us the way as though he'd figured out the best route to get us safely back to my sister's house. Maybe it was how quiet the world seemed just then when snow had frozen most of the Mid-atlantic and Northeast coast. Icy crystals sparkled in the crisp air, and the thick snow hushed every sound. I could imagine for a little while that no one else existed—only us in our snow globe world.

But when we made it back to my sister's house, the spell was broken. Another car was now parked in the driveway. Keisha speculated that it was probably my cousins.

But this car was too high-end for any of them. I was almost sure it was April's parents.

18

KEISHA - MAKING AMENDS

Ellie was wrong. The snow didn't keep everyone away. We barely had a chance to hang up our coats before Ellie called for Nick to come to the kitchen.

"Go, I'll be there in a minute." I crouched down to unclip Rufus's leash from his collar. Nick lingered, though. He crouched beside me and took the opportunity to give Rufus an affectionate pat.

"I have the feeling I'm about to get a surprise." Nick sounded cautious. He'd tensed in the driveway, but I thought it was just due to how slippery it was in some spots.

Ellie called for him again. Now, she came out into the hallway. She was fidgety and the anxious expression she wore made both Nick and me a little nervous. The mouthwatering aroma of sage, onions, and butter, mixed with turkey, was already spreading in the air. My stomach grumbled in protest. We hadn't eaten breakfast yet. If Ellie already had guests, maybe it was better if I went out. We'd passed a café during our walk. It was open for business despite the weather.

"Is it your cousins?"

"Don't stay away, Keisha." Nick stood to his full height. He held his hand out to me, and I stood too.

"I'm just going to..." I gestured at the stairs. I didn't even know what I wanted from upstairs, but I knew I didn't want to walk into that kitchen unprepared. And whoever was in there with Ellie would want to see Nick first. I eased my hand from his and escaped up the stairs. Once I was in our bedroom, I sank down onto the bed and tried to remind myself that Nick and I didn't need to be afraid of what anyone else thought.

———

ELLIE, NICK, AND APRIL'S PARENTS WERE IN THE KITCHEN WHEN I came back downstairs. At the bottom of the stairs, I waited. Should I join them? I thought I would know what to do, but now, doubt had crept in. Their voices were hushed, though; a few times I hung back, feeling a little like an intruder. Instead, I crossed the hall into the living room. Ellie was one of those women who liked to start decorating for the holidays early. She'd already draped fragrant boughs of pine across the mantlepiece crowning her fireplace. A ceramic Nativity scene was nestled among the pine needles.

Built-in bookcases framed either side of the fireplace. Every shelf was filled with books and knick-knacks. Someone had lit a fire, and Rufus was taking advantage of it. He'd curled up in front of it and fallen asleep. His canine snoring brought a smile to my lips. I took my phone from the back pocket of my jeans and snapped a picture of him napping there. I would show it to Nick later.

On the coffee table was a leather-bound photo album. "Our Family" was embossed on the front in dull, gold script. I hadn't noticed it before, but then again...I'd barely spent time in the living room last night. We'd gone directly into the kitchen to warm up and eat, and then I'd gone upstairs to give Nick and his sister some time on their own. While they talked, I'd curled up in the window seat in the bedroom and read a book on my Kindle while listening to music with my headphones.

My curiosity got the better of me. I eased down onto the sofa and flipped open the album. The first picture I was greeted with was a younger, happier version of Nick, clad in a tuxedo and looking a little drunk...on wine, on love. His hair was slicked down and the beard I'd grown so used to was nowhere in sight. April was in his arms, her face turned up to his, tendrils of blond curls escaping from her upswept hairdo, but she didn't seem to care. In the background, the black cherry trees in Bryan Park's Japanese garden were in full bloom.

I turned the pages, more wedding pictures, and then Nick holding a swaddled baby. Underneath it, someone had written: "You will be the best father in the world." Next to it, a little note read, "Caitlin - 5 hours old".

I continued studying the pictures, evidence of his life before me, before Rufus even. In some of them, Nick looked bewildered, as if asking himself how he'd ended up where he was; in others, he seemed so happy that it made me smile too. His first Christmas as a dad, Audrey's arrival into the little family, April's birthday celebration, and the girls' first days at school.

I was nearly at the end, but now in these photos, Nick smiled less, sometimes he'd been caught looking in the opposite direction, especially in the pictures when he and April were together. They'd gone from being nearly inseparable to being captured on film with an ocean of others between them— sometimes, the children; sometimes, other family members. But they'd loved one another, and I had the feeling that if he could turn back time, he would. People married for better or for worse, even if not everyone took those vows seriously.

"Hey..."

I nearly started. I shove the book away. Nick stood in the archway, his forearm resting against the doorsill.

"You're sitting here alone." Nick rubbed his chin through his thick beard. "Come join us in the kitchen."

"Your parents-in-law are here." It sounded so silly, but the truth of the matter was that I didn't want to intrude on their chance to reconcile. I wasn't a party to it. "You should be in there...not here."

"I know, but... I didn't want you to be alone."

His words and the shy, boyish smile he flashed sent a flurry of joy through me. I'd never felt like this with Alex or any of the other men I'd dated. Maybe I'd always rushed into things with the others. With them, we'd never taken the time to get to know one another. There never really seemed to be a reason for it— when my world revolved around dance and they only wanted someone to fuck. So many times, that was all I wanted, to fill a void, to not feel anything.

"I've got Rufus...even if he is asleep."

"Yeah, he snores a lot, doesn't he?" Nick came over to the sofa. His tone was gentle as he spoke.

"You looked so happy..."

"We were," he said softly. "For a while. Toward the end, things weren't rosy. I can admit that now."

"Is that what you write in your notebook?"

"It helps." When we sat together like this, I could imagine being with him for the rest of my life. I envied April for the time she'd had with him. Even when he told me he was not the world's best husband, I thought he was being too hard on himself. No one on this earth could claim to be perfect. We all had our selfish moments. I was having one now. I wanted to keep him by my side, but he couldn't avoid his former in-laws.

"You should go back to the kitchen." I couldn't stop myself from stroking the back of his neck. His skin was so soft and his hair slightly curled there. "It's okay, I'll be fine here with Rufus."

"I'd rather stay here with you."

"I'll be here for you. You know that."

"Don't ever disappear on me."

"Not likely to happen," I assured him and took advantage of the moment to kiss him and silence any doubts and fears within him.

He kissed me again, light enough to feel like a promise, long enough to leave me wanting more before he gave in and returned to the kitchen. Their voices drifted down the hall. I could have joined them. In a way, I wanted to, but he needed to get through this on his own, even if he didn't know it.

He needed to make amends with the past.

19

NICK: THE PAST IS FORGIVEN, NOT FORGOTTEN

"We don't blame you, Nick." Emily, April's mother, held my hand in a tight grip. "It's important that you know this. We don't blame you for any of what happened."

Ellie had left us alone in the kitchen. The Christmas carols playing softly in the background made an incongruous sound-track for this moment. William, April's father, nodded in agreement at his wife's words. In the five years since I'd last seen them, they'd both aged. William's hair had gone completely grey and was thinning out near his temples. His face, too, was thinner and more drawn now.

"That's not what you said before."

"We were grieving, Nick. We were angry and confused." William spoke now, his voice shaky and low. "Emily and I said things we should have never, ever said. And we spoke out of anger. We'd lost our only child. Our beautiful granddaughters..."

"And I lost my wife and my children. I lost everything in

that moment." Those words summed up all the frustration and anger in me. I tried to draw my hand back, but Emily wouldn't let go. "I lost everything. I lost my grasp on the world when they died."

"But look at you now, Nick." Emily squeezed my hand. "You are in love again. Please don't think that we don't want you to be alone."

"We want you to have a life." William's eyes were glassy. In all the years that April and I were married, I'd never seen William so vulnerable or emotional. "We're so sorry that we ever blamed you for what happened that night."

The kitchen timer began to ring, breaking the tense mood. Emily released my hand and then stood and went to the stove. She checked the turkey and basted it with the pan juices. I stood too. I needed something to do, something to distract me from the confusion inside of me. I'd held on too long to the resentment I'd harbored toward Emily and William for the misplaced blame they'd placed on me. I rummaged through the cupboards, found the electric kettle, and began making tea.

I didn't even like tea very much, but it seemed like something to do.

William came to my side. His presence reminded me of the calm I'd felt when my father used to stand beside and watch over me as I worked on a model train or my homework. Now, William was here, pulling cups and saucers from a wall cabinet. He hummed bits of a Christmas carol to himself then realized what he was doing and shook his head.

"Will your girlfriend join us for tea?"

I nodded then croaked, "Yeah, yeah...I think she'd like that."

I didn't want Keisha to feel that she could not be here with us. She'd helped me through so much during these last few months, helped me to see life through eyes not clouded by my grief and guilt.

"I'll go and get her then, son." William gave my shoulder a reassuring pat. "I want to hear about how you two met."

"It's a good story." I found Ellie's tin of Christmas tea and her favorite Christmas teapot. She'd inherited our mom's passion for seasonal decorating, though, when we were younger, she hated all of this. Ellie used to complain about the fuss Mom made about having the right seasonal flag or the size of the Thanksgiving centerpiece.

Emily took over helping me. While she filled the tea infusers, I gave her the details of how Keisha and I met.

"It sounds almost too good to be true." Emily found a tray we could use to bring everything over to the table. "It's like something from a Hollywood movie—a rainy, summer night... two people destined to meet."

"It is kind of like a movie, isn't it?" I grinned. "I'm pretty sure the universe wanted us to cross paths."

"I'm so glad that Ellie told me you were coming," she continued our conversation without missing a beat. "When you left Boston, I truly believed you'd only be gone for a short while. Perhaps a few months."

"I couldn't stay in that house without them."

"No, I understand that now. At the time, I thought you were running away from your guilt."

"I was running away."

"No, my dear, you were grieving. I understand that now. You'd had a horrible, horrible shock." Emily spoke in a low, calm manner. She reminded me a little of Dr. Sheridan. "For you to come home to the police..." her voice trailed off.

Emily set a steadying hand on the edge of the counter. I'd lifted the heavy tray, but now I put it back down on the counter and comforted my former mother-in-law as she began to sob. The trickle of tears streaked her perfectly made-up face.

"Oh for heaven's sake. I didn't think I would break down like this."

We'd never done these things once we finally accepted that April, Caitlin, and Audrey were never coming back to us. We'd dwelled so long in the land of the dead.

We'd forgotten that we could go on living. Emily's shoulders shook with each sob she tried to hold in. She finally let go, and her tears flowed freely. I kept my arms around her shoulders. It wasn't long ago when a news story could remind me of that night, and I'd turn to a bottle of whiskey to dull the pain.

"I saw you from the window." Emily wiped at her tears with the back of her shaky hand. "You were holding her hand, making sure she didn't slip on any ice. It reminded me of that first time April brought you home for Thanksgiving. Do you remember?"

"The ice storm... we nearly fell on the steps to the front door."

"And you caught April without even thinking about stopping your own fall, and you broke your arm."

"We spent a couple of hours in ER."

"Thank God we could pull a few strings, so you didn't have to sit all day waiting for a doctor."

I'd nearly forgotten about that. I'd arrived at the hospital at around the same time as three ambulances with car crash victims. Their condition was rightly deemed by the nurses on duty to be far more severe than mine. I accepted it, but neither April nor her parents would. No one wanted to delay dinner just because of a little ice storm or my broken arm. William had a friend from his golfing circle who happened to be the chief of surgery at the hospital. It only took a phone call to get me out of the queue of lower priority patients and into a treatment room, getting my arm x-rayed, splinted, and in a partial cast. It didn't take long before we were back at April's parents' house and Thanksgiving could continue as usual.

Emily composed herself enough to find a Thanksgiving-themed paper napkin to blot her tears. She folded it carefully and inserted it into her pocket. I took the opportunity to move the tea tray to the kitchen table.

"I'm glad you've found love again, Nick," Emily said after a while. "I think April, Caitlyn, and Audrey would be glad too."

20

KEISHA - 'TIS THE SEASON

One of my favorite things about living in the Museum District was how the residents seemed to live and breathe for Christmas. Every house I passed on my way home from Le Pêche was decorated with holiday finery. Nets of white lights draped hedges and shrubs. Huge wreaths hung on front doors, and colorful lights lined porch railings and rooflines. I took longer than usual to walk home so that I could enjoy the sights.

We'd been home from Boston for a little over a week. Nick seemed more relaxed. Lately, I even caught him whistling. Even Rufus was confounded by that development. We were so used to Nick never listening to music, to the long periods of silence when he'd keep to himself and avoid the neighbors. But sometimes, I even caught him chatting with the O'Neils who lived next door, and he'd even invited Olivia and Hannes to come over for holiday drinks.

Tonight, I slowed down as I came closer to the house—instead of the usual darkness cut by only the light from the window—the front of the house glowed from the strings of white Christmas lights lining the porch roof and railings; pine boughs strung with lights framed the front door and LED candles were set in every window.

"It's lovely, isn't it?" Mrs. Ferguson, who lived a few houses away, marveled as she came to a stop beside me. The older woman was bundled in a puffy red down jacket and sheepskin boots. Her bluish-grey hair formed a fluffy halo on her head. She tugged on the retractable leashes controlling her rambunctious chihuahuas, Zorro and Pedro. "All the years I've known Nicholas, he's never decorated before."

"No, I didn't think he would, but this is great." I moved my foot before Pedro lifted his leg to relieve himself.

"He smiles so much more these days." Mrs. Ferguson sounded pleased. I could hear the surprise and happiness in her voice. "Mrs. O'Neil and I have kept an eye on him since he moved in, making sure he was all right, trying to get him to open up. He was always friendly, but he was distant."

Zorro yipped and pranced, anxious to continue his walk and read the pee-mail. Pedro joined him, not ready to be outdone by his brother chihuahua.

"Oh, the boys are ready to go." Mrs. Ferguson clicked the leashes again and patted my arm. "Tell Nick we think the house just looks wonderful."

She let the dogs pull her along the sidewalk to continue the rest of their evening walk.

———

I BARELY HAD A CHANCE TO TAKE OFF MY COAT BEFORE NICK gathered me in his arms and claimed me with deep kisses that had me ready to strip right there in the entryway. I slid my hand inside his shirt and let his body heat warm my palm. I loved how his arms felt around me. He was so strong and unafraid to show his affection. He made me feel loved in a way that was brand new for me.

"Let's go upstairs..." I was already unbuttoning his shirt, but he stopped me.

"We can't..."

"Why...? I can tell you want me."

"Your parents are here." His lips hovered over mine, teasing me even as he murmured that they were upstairs resting before we went out to dinner. "So, you need to change... and we should probably stop kissing..."

"You'll have to stop kissing me then," I teased and nipped his lower lip. "But later, you're mine."

21

NICK - NEVER LET ME GO

"Nicholas, I think it's time." Dr. Sheridan raised her teacup to her lips. "I think you're aware of this as well."

"Yeah, I am." I was sitting in my usual chair at my therapist's office, grasping my notebook of memories in my hands. The pebbled cover was a little warped now from all the times I'd sat on it or Rufus insisted on carrying it in his mouth. It probably smelled a little like canine drool. "I never thought I would get to this point."

For five years, I'd been trying to work my way out of what had been the darkest, loneliest period of my life. I'd written everything down, all of my guilt, the times I'd let my wife down or when I spent evenings drinking beer and watching baseball games in pubs instead of coming home to my daughters. I'd also written down the good times—how awestruck I was by my newborn daughters, how I looked forward to reading to them at bedtime during the brief time I had them in my life.

I flipped open the notebook and scanned the words I'd written. So many times, I'd crossed out whole paragraphs that sounded too critical of April or me, especially in the beginning. Those were the hardest months and years. When the wounds were still fresh. When I still thought I could retrace my steps and somehow undo that horrible night when I'd lost April and the kids.

Was it weird to sit here in this armchair in an office decorated for Christmas and Hanukkah? I'd noticed it when I first arrived—the menorah on the mantlepiece nestled with silver and gold sprayed pinecones, the wreath decorated with bells and ribbons used as a centerpiece on her coffee table, two more hanging in the windows of her office. I couldn't remember ever seeing her office decorated for the holidays in all the years I'd been coming to see her.

"Nicholas...shall we do it together now?" Dr. Sheridan repeated her question. I'd been so distracted I missed it the first time.

"I'd rather do it at home." I had to consider it for a while. I'd known this day would come, when I would understand that I no longer needed to write in my journal to remind myself of what had happened, of what I'd lost, or what lay ahead of me.

"You should be proud of yourself, Nicholas," Dr. Sheridan took another sip of her clove-scented tea. "You've worked through everything that held you back. You accepted that you are not to blame for what happened to your wife and your children. You've let go of your guilt. You've moved forward with your life."

Listening to her recount everything I'd gone through only clarified the progress I'd made. Even just a few months ago, I'd still blamed myself for what happened to April and the girls. It wasn't until I finally began taking Dr. Sheridan's homework seriously...and began talking about that night with Keisha that it all started to feel less like my fault and more like a horrible stroke of bad luck.

"I don't need to hold onto these memories anymore," I said. "So, tonight, I'll let go of them completely."

———

THE FRESH BALSAM SCENT OF PINE BOUGHS AND CHRIS REA'S raspy voice singing "Driving Home for Christmas" greeted me as I walked through the front door. A potted amaryllis plant stood on the catchall table in the hall. Its vibrant red blooms seemed almost too showy and sexy for Christmas, but somehow, they felt right for us. A silver lantern with a thick church candle inside kept the flower company on the table and helped set the holiday mood.

A trio of voices drifted into the hallway from the kitchen. Keisha's parents had returned from sightseeing in DC and Christmas shopping, and Rufus, who usually came out to greet me, was too distracted even to notice I'd come home. I didn't mind. It had been a while since coming home felt like a good thing. I'd spent so many years in my private underworld with nothing but guilt, anger, and ghosts as companions. I'd never believed Ellie when she said there would come a time when I'd come back to the light. She'd been so sure, even when I'd sunk so low that I didn't think I could ever return to a world where love meant anything.

I was happy, in love, and actually excited about what the future had in store for me.

It all started because of a chance meeting on a rainy night at the Staples Mill Road train station. Where would I be now if I hadn't stopped that night when I saw her standing in the rain?

———

LATER, ONCE KEISHA'S PARENTS HAD SETTLED IN FOR THE EVENING in the guest bedroom at the back of the house, I lit a fire in the fireplace, relaxed on the sofa, and waited for Keisha to return from the ballet studio. She'd gone to help with Olivia and Johannes with some of the final preparations for tomorrow's performance at the Museum of Art.

I'd taken her parents out to dinner at La Pêche and gotten to know them a little better.

Beside me, Rufus snored, his legs twitching now and then. Maybe he was dreaming about chasing a Christmas ham. We had enough food in the house now. Keisha's mom had filled the freezer with plastic containers full of Christmas cookies. Last night, she'd glazed and baked a ham and prepped a sweet potato casserole that she said we only needed to pop in the oven on Christmas Day.

The house was quiet, but it didn't feel empty. There was a warmth now that it had lacked. The ghosts of my past had finally been laid to rest.

I glanced at my phone to check the time. It was getting late —nearly midnight—and Keisha wasn't home yet. I had to remind myself that she knew how to take care of herself, but that didn't stop me from worrying. Ever since the election, there'd been a palpable shift in attitude that left me a little uneasy. Some neighbors were no longer as friendly as they'd once been. A few hung confederate flags on their front porches. Even though our neighborhood was relatively quiet, I didn't like the idea of her walking home by herself late at night.

Above me, the floorboards creaked. Keisha's mother appeared at the top of the stairs. "Has she come home yet?" she asked, her voice full of concern.

"Not yet." I was already on my feet. "I thought I'd drive over to the studio and meet her."

"Thank you for doing this, Nick."

"It's no problem, honestly. It's too late for her to walk home on her own." I went over to the vestibule and grabbed my parka from the coatrack. Maddie was dressed in a plum velour tracksuit she'd called her loungewear and canvas sneakers. "Do you want to come with me?"

"I don't want to get in the way..."

"It's no problem." I nodded at Rufus, who was still snoring on the couch. "My usual partner's fallen asleep."

We drove to the studio, even though it wasn't very far. The nights were frigid now, and the sidewalks slippery with frost and ice. With so many rehearsals and late nights at La Pêche, Keisha was coming home later than before.

On the way there, Maddie told me about the first time Keisha asked to take ballet lessons. "She was so determined. She's always been that way. Walter and I...we knew she'd seen a ballet on TV, but we didn't think she'd be so obsessed with it."

"When you see her dance, you'll understand why she fought so hard to do it."

I'd parked across the street from Hannes and Olivia's dance studio. The warm glow of the studio's lights cut through the winter darkness. Maddie adjusted her scarf as we crossed the street. She stopped in front of the studio and watched as her daughter danced.

Keisha was dressed in her favorite practice gear—pale pink leggings, slouchy grey leg warmers that had probably seen better days, and a leotard that was nearly the same shade as her golden-brown skin, layered with one of my plaid flannel shirts which she'd tied in a knot at her waist. She closed her eyes as she danced and let her senses roam free. I'd seen her do this before in the evenings when I came by the studio. She swore when she did this she could feel the music on her skin, guiding her and allowing her to become one with it.

Maddie and I watched from outside. Olivia waved for us to come inside, but neither of us wanted to disturb the moment. Even with her knee injury, Keisha danced beautifully. Maddie was transfixed. Her eyes widened in surprise as she watched her daughter en pointe, her slender arms fluttering like a bird's wings as she moved from one attitude to the next.

I guided Maddie inside, hoping our entry wouldn't distract Keisha.

I nodded at Hannes and Olivia, who were waiting for their cues to join Keisha. Every movement she made seemed so delicate yet revealed the control she wielded over her body. I'd watched her practice this scene so often—the final waltz. She moved so effortlessly, as though the swells of music that Tchaikovsky had composed bedazzled her and carried her in their waves.

Maddie clutched my hand, squeezing it as the waltz came to a close. She only let go of my hand to show her appreciation in applause. I joined her. I loved watching Keisha dance, loved catching her by surprise when she'd been so lost in the music and the dance that she didn't notice anything else.

"I had no idea she was so good," Maddie murmured, her admiration evident in her voice. "All those years..." She relaxed, but her smile never wavered. The love and admiration she had for Keisha burned so brightly. Maybe now she'd let it shine more instead of hiding it.

"The first time I saw her dance...it made me wish I knew how to dance too. I wanted to dance to the edge of time with her." Even now as we sat down to watch, the longing to be there with her, extending my hand to her as she pirouetted, wishing I could be her partner in dance and life was as strong as that first time when I'd watched her dance with Hannes.

"I'm going to marry your daughter." The words came naturally to me. "One day soon. I'm going to ask her to marry me. And I think she'll say yes. I'm going to spend the rest of my life with her."

———

ONCE WE WERE HOME, MADDIE AND KEISHA TALKED OVER A POT of tea, while I relaxed in the living room and read. They needed this—a chance to reconnect without their own ghosts of the past clouding them. Their laughter made me smile. It meant things were improving. Maddie had seen Keisha in a new light. Tomorrow, when her father would be able to see her dance for the first time, it would be a revelation for him as well.

I nodded to myself. Now felt right. A newly awakened Rufus watched as I went over to the fireplace. He cocked his head to the side and let out a curious bark.

"Hush, Rufus." I pulled my notebook of memories out of my back pocket. It was time to let it go. Rufus hopped down from the sofa and came to my side. He nudged my hand with his wet nose.

I murmured goodbye to the weight of the past. I tossed the book into the flames and watched it burn. I would always love April, Caitlin, and Audrey. And that was okay. I loved them and still had room in my heart to move on and rediscover love with Keisha.

I loved her. And that was all that mattered now.

ABOUT THE AUTHOR

Kim Golden is a *USA Today* bestselling author of romantic fiction. Born and raised in the City of Brotherly Love, Kim left the US in 1995 and moved to Sweden for love with a capital L. When she isn't writing fiction featuring smart, beautiful African American women and sexy Scandinavians, she moonlights as a copywriter for a pretty famous Swedish furniture brand.

She writes stories for people who know that love comes in every color.

Sign up for her newsletter to be the first to hear about new releases, promotions, and exclusive giveaways. Or join her review team if you're crazy about her books and want to help Kim spread the word.

Follow Kim or drop her a line:
kim-golden.com
kim@kim-golden.com

ACKNOWLEDGMENTS

There are so many people who've been in my corner as I tried to get back on track after a particularly rough period in my life. I was afraid that I'd lost my writing mojo forever but these angels helped me rediscover my path to storytelling.

To all of the members of In the Zone with Kim Golden, thank you so much for hanging in there with me through thick and thin. I am so grateful for and appreciative of all the love and support you've all shown me through these last few years. I don't know what I would have done without you.

Grazie to my Matera Brainstormers. For so many years, you've been my tribe of writers who've helped me work through story ideas and tackle all of my bouts of writer's block. You were there for me when my father died and helped me get through it. And you were there for me when my brother died and I thought I might never write another book. I hope we'll be able to meet again soon for days of brainstorming and enjoying *la dolce vita.*

To my small but wonderful group of beta readers and

reviewers. Thanks so much for hanging in there with me and for always having constructive critique to help me grow as a writer.

Many hugs and lots of love to Beate, Caroline, Sonata, Erika, Lisette, Rasmus, Anna Y., Erik, Anna H., and Alex G. for being my support network when all of us were going through a hell of a time at the Big O. We kept each other sane, had the best *fikas* and made it through.

A gazillion thanks to Patrice from Little Pear Editing. You are always there for me and I truly appreciate how you always find a way to make time for me, even when your schedule is super busy. Your enthusiasm for my stories is one of the things that keeps me writing.

To Tiffanie, Fiona and Ashley for our long chats over wine and nosh whenever I am in Philadelphia. I live for those times and hate that the pandemic has kept us from being able to explore Philly's restaurant scene together.

To all of the writers (here in Europe and the US) who also happen to be my friends who've been a great support to me as I was going through the grieving process and trying to find my way again. You know who are and I love you all for giving me strength when I didn't always have it.

And, finally, to my noisy muse. Thank you for everything you do to give me space and time to write, for interrupting me for kisses and Prosecco (which I love, by the way), and never losing faith in me...even when I didn't always have it.

Kim

ALSO BY KIM GOLDEN

Maybe... series

Maybe Baby

Maybe Tonight

Maybe Baby: Special Edition - the Laney & Mads Collection

Maybe Forever

Maybe Tomorrow

Other Books

Under the Midnight Sun

Snowbound

Choose Me: a novella

Linger: a short story

www.ingramcontent.com/pod-product-compliance
Lightning Source LLC
Chambersburg PA
CBHW030312200626
46816CB00002BA/868